THANK YOU
To my critique group:
Connie Morgenstern, Susan Manzke, Pam Kuck, Mary Guhl.

DEDICATION
To my parents
Ruth Lillian Mohr Nehrlich
and
Raymond Hugo Nehrlich,
great-great-grandson of the immigrants,
heir to the pitcher.

The Immigrants' Chronicles

FROM GERMANY TO AMERICA

THE JOURNEY OF
Emilie

MARCIA HOEHNE

Chariot Victor Publishing
A Division of Cook Communications

Be sure to read all the books in
The Immigrants' Chronicles

The Journey of Emilie
The Journey of Hannah
The Journey of Pieter and Anna

Chariot Victor Publishing
a division of Cook Communications, Colorado Springs, Colorado 80918
Cook Communications, Paris, Ontario
Kingsway Communications, Eastbourne, England

THE JOURNEY OF EMILIE
© 1999 by Marcia Hoehne

Edited by Kathy Davis
Cover design by PAZ Design Group
Art direction by Andrea Boven
Cover illustration by Cheri Bladholm

First printing, 1999
Printed in the United States of America
03 02 01 00 99   5 4 3 2 1

Library of Congress Cataloging-in-Publication Data

Hoehne, Marcia, 1951-
    The journey of Emilie / Marcia Hoehne.
    p. cm. — (The immigrants chronicles)
    "From Germany to America."
    SUMMARY: After traveling from Germany to settle in Wisconsin,
Emilie's family finds life hard until they find a mysterious stash of
money hidden in their china pitcher.
    ISBN 0-7814-3081-X
    I. Title. II. Series.
    PZ7.H667 Jo 1999
    [Fic] — ddc21

                                                        98-35697
                                                            CIP
                                                             AC

Chapter One

RURAL GOTHA, THURINGEN, CENTRAL GERMANY, AUGUST 1855

"*Nordamerika?*"

Twelve-year-old Emilie Borner jumped at her brother's shout, dropping her chunk of rye bread onto her plate. As Karl leaped from his chair and towered over Papa, Emilie stared.

"You're going to emigrate? *Auswandern?*" Karl repeated the word.

"This is news to you?" chided Otto, age ten, gnawing at his bread. "Papa's been wanting to leave for a year."

"Farm owners don't emigrate!"

Papa's eyes met Karl's. "Did you really convince yourself that this was idle talk? Our emigration papers are in order. The farm is for sale."

"Well, I'm staying," Karl declared. "I'll board at the cooper shop full-time." At nineteen, Karl worked for a barrel maker.

"We have a ticket for you," Papa replied. "We sail in four weeks."

Emilie knew this should end the matter, for no unmarried child was independent until age twenty-one.

But Karl turned his blue-eyed gaze on Mama. "You've never wanted to leave. You've said so."

Emilie, too, switched her attention to Mama, who had never liked talk of a New World. She believed a New World would come only with Christ's return. "We mustn't be like Abraham," Mama had once said. "He got impatient waiting for the son God promised him, so he fathered Ishmael. It brought his people no end of trouble." She had shaken her head. "I, for one, intend to wait for God's promise."

But now, seeing Mama's peaceful face, Emilie realized she would hear something different. "I've had a year to think and to pray." Mama's faded blue eyes implored Karl to understand. "What sin is there in crossing the ocean? We don't ask for a life of ease, only a chance to work for a living." A faint smile touched Mama's lips. "I recall quoting an example from the life of Abraham. Here's another one: When God prompted Abraham to leave his country for a new land, Abraham went."

Karl faced Papa again. "You've cowed her into going. You dredged up a Bible story to use to your advantage."

Emilie had had enough. "Papa has never treated Mama that way," she cried. "Mama knows her own mind. So do I," she added, just to quell any ideas Karl might have about mindless women.

Papa's face had reddened dangerously. Karl took a deep breath and relaxed his fists. "Papa, the political situation is better now. Duke Ernest wants a united Germany and a German parliament. He supports the Jews. His ideas are spreading through the German states. There'll be another move for democracy, don't you see?"

Papa motioned to Karl's chair. Karl sat.

"Since you see fit to address me man-to-man," Papa said, "I'll do the same. It's not only about politics. It's about survival—about a future for your brother and sister . . . and you."

"A future for Otto?" Karl challenged. "You've put his future up for sale!"

Emilie knew Karl meant the farm. It was her family's custom, and the custom of other families in Thuringen, to pass farmland to the youngest son. Even Martin Luther's family, living nearby more than 300 years ago, had practiced this custom.

"I'm not talking about the manhood of a boy barely ten," Papa said. "The future we must think of now is nearer than ever before."

Mama leaned toward Karl. "Son, do you see the cabbage on your plate?"

6

Karl's strong jaw hardened, and he stared unseeing at the tabletop. Most of the dark, homespun tablecloth was visible, because only the bowl of cabbage sat there.

"What is it about the cabbage?" Mama persisted. She shined her pale eyes on Emilie, then Otto. "I want you children to understand."

Emilie glanced at her shreds of boiled cabbage and lifted her face to Mama's. "It hasn't been made into sauerkraut."

"Exactly." Mama nodded. "And why did we make cabbage into sauerkraut?"

"Because sauerkraut smells good and tastes better," Otto piped up. "Why couldn't this cabbage be sauerkraut, my nose wants to know?" He sniffed deeply. He had always gulped big breaths when meals included sauerkraut. Emilie realized she hadn't had to eat with the noisy breathing for some time. Clearly, a spurt of maturity on Otto's part was not the reason.

Mama spoke. "We make cabbage into sauerkraut so it doesn't spoil. So it will keep."

"And we no longer have enough cabbage to put by." The instant she spoke the words, Emilie wished she could swallow them. No one had ever said aloud that food was dwindling.

"It's not complaining to speak the truth, *Liebchen*," Papa said softly. He faced Karl again. "We're not starving. But shall we wait until we are? Now we're thin. Shall we wait until we're weak, maybe sick? Now Ernst has money to buy me out. Shall we wait until no one can afford land?"

"Herr Conrad is buying the farm?" exclaimed Emilie. If the Conrads, the tenant family who farmed with the Borners, were going to buy the farm, then her best friend, Louise Conrad, was staying while she was going. A pang of dismay struck Emilie.

Karl's thoughts seemed similar. "If we should get out, why is it all right for Herr Conrad to stay, and to give you his money in the bargain?"

"You think I've hoodwinked my friend somehow?" Papa asked. "Ernst is convinced the farm can support one family until times are better. He won't leave his aged mother, who is too ill to face an ocean voyage. The truth is, Karl," Papa said, "Ernst believes God is calling his family to stay. Just as He's calling ours to go."

Karl looked grim. "That always ends the discussion, doesn't it? God says do this; God says do that. And it's settled."

"Have I refused to discuss my decision with you, Karl? Have I refused to give reasons?"

"How can I know," Karl asked quietly, "when someone has heard from God or when he's closing his mind?"

A hush came over the table. "All I can advise, son," Papa said, "is that you draw close to God yourself. Come to know Him better yourself."

The silence lengthened. Mama broke it. "Why don't you read us the America letter, Franz? It helps to hear how others are getting on in the new land."

A letter from America? Emilie sat at attention. She loved America letters.

"This is from Heinrich Schulz." Papa drew a letter from his pocket and unfolded it. "Since leaving last year, he has settled near a place called . . ." Papa checked the envelope. "Sheboygan, Wisconsin. He says this is inland, but is a bustling lake port, surrounded by good farmland."

Herr Schulz's letter told of abundant corn and wheat crops and the birth of a new baby, "'An American citizen from his first breath, though I also now have the vote, after one year's residence in Wisconsin. It is good here, friend. No registering with police, no titles of nobility, no beggars.'"

No titles? Emilie wondered. No dukes and grand dukes and princes, all better than herself? And no beggars? No out-of-work craftsmen roaming for a bite of bread, or crowded tenant farmers scratching vegetables from tiny plots? She cast a glance at her cabbage, deciding to take a forkful.

"'Food aboard ship may be meager,'" Papa read. "'I advise you to bring zwieback, dried meat, and prunes. Also vinegar, which will be useful . . .'" Papa's voice died away.

"Which will be useful how, Franz?" Mama prompted.

"'To mix with the smelly drinking water,'" Papa finished. Karl snorted.

"'By all means share this letter,'" Papa continued, "'with the Albrechts and Jurgens who will travel with you.'"

Consternation filled Emilie. The Albrechts and Jurgens? Oh, Emilie loved sweet little Heidi Jurgen, but the Albrechts? Snoopy, snooty Rosamund Albrecht, who boasted of riches and claimed kinship to Duke Ernest, was going to America with her? America suddenly seemed anything but vast and green. America suddenly sounded small indeed.

* * *

After washing the supper dishes, Emilie slipped outside into the August evening. The sun still blazed yellow. A warm wind flared her simple brown skirt and teased the stray ringlets that escaped her brown braids. Turning back and forth and around, she studied her homeland.

To the north and east, small farms like hers were tucked among rolling hills. In the south and west, Emilie's eyes traced plateaus rising to mountain peaks and thick trees in the Thuringian Forest. Beyond the forest, she knew, the Werra River rose, flowing north to the broadening Weser and on to the sea.

Despite recent poor crops and boundary lines and tariffs that made economic life hard, Emilie couldn't imagine leaving home forever. A lump formed in her throat.

"Emilie!"

Emilie spun around to greet her best friend, Louise Conrad, who trotted toward her from the smaller home on the Borner farm. Her dark blond hair loosening from its ribbon, Louise stopped short and met Emilie's blue eyes with her own. "I can't believe you are going to America."

"I can't believe America is real," Emilie answered slowly. "When people leave for America, it's like—"

"They are disappearing into eternity," Louise finished.

Both girls fell silent, thinking about this.

"Of course, it's not really eternity," Louise said.

"The America letters make it sound wonderful, but not like heaven," agreed Emilie. She remembered Mama's warning against searching for a New World on earth, and shivered.

"Speaking of America letters, we had one today," Louise said. "It told how some people go on sailing ships, and others on steamships. And how you ride either in cabins or in a place called steerage. It said much depends on the weather."

"Much—?"

Louise rolled her lips together, as if sorry she'd started this. "How fast you get there depends on the weather. How seasick people get depends on the weather."

"Oh," said Emilie.

The girls began to stroll toward the barn. "Mama wonders if America has Reformed churches," Louise went on. "She says what if you have to go to the *lutherisch* or the *katholisch?* She says—"

"Oh, that won't be a problem," Emilie interrupted. Much as she loved occasional gossip with Louise, lately it bothered her. Mama, too, had exclaimed how tired she was of petty, idle talk.

"This one bribed his way into the Duke's inner circle, but he's a traitor," Mama had recited. "That one ran off to university, leaving two girls doomed to spinsterhood. This one renounced Christianity to become a Free Thinker. That one says the steel industry is headed for disaster, the boundaries are in dispute again, English imports will drive us to the poorhouse, and on and on. How can we love our neighbors when our tongues flap with lies and criticism?" Maybe, Emilie reflected, constant gossip was another reason Mama was willing to leave.

"What do you mean, it won't be a problem?" Louise demanded.

"W—What?" Emilie asked, jerked from her daydream. They rounded a corner of the barn.

"If there's no Reformed church in America?"

"But there must be," said Emilie. "And if not, we'd help start one. In America, people are rich and free. Land is plentiful and cheap. Even if you don't believe the pamphlets and leaflets that praise Wisconsin to the skies, surely the America letters don't lie."

Louise took her time replying. "I see how much you want to go. I shall miss you, Emilie Borner."

Emilie might have protested that her feelings were mixed. She might have pointed out that Louise's family would own the farm now, and move into the bigger house. She might even have willed her bedroom to Louise, but that thought made her eyes tear up and her throat ache. It would never do to use the word *will*, as if she really were headed into eternity. Besides, Louise would have to share a room with her sisters or her grandmother. So Emilie said nothing. As they approached the next corner of the barn, Louise, too, kept silent.

"I tell you, Erich." Karl's voice, hushed but rough, suddenly burst from around the corner ahead of them. Emotions forgotten, the two friends stopped dead in their tracks.

"My father thinks we may yet be sent to fight the Crimean war," Karl continued hoarsely. "I say we will not. And if we are, I am not afraid."

"*Ach*, war," scoffed Karl's companion. Emilie knew he was Erich Jurgen, son of the Jurgens who were to travel with them. "I am going to university here. How can Papa think some wilderness school would substitute for Heidelberg or Göttingen?"

"Or Jena," hissed Karl. "I want to join the *Burschenschaft*. Even if it has gone underground, we'll find it at Jena. It was founded there."

Emilie wasn't sure what the *Burschenschaft* was. Knowing Karl, she decided it must be a political group that favored a united Germany.

"I tell you, Erich," Karl repeated. "Of this I am sure: I am not going to America."

Chapter Two

Whenever Karl appeared at the farmhouse to argue with Papa, Emilie longed to push her family's departure far into the future. At other times, stooping in the garden to pick stunted cucumbers or pry withered potatoes from the ground, she yearned to sail away to a new life. Finally the last Sunday in August arrived, hot and sunny. On this afternoon of the travelers' farewell party, uplifted by good news from Karl, Emilie danced into the kitchen with a sense of adventure.

Rap, rap-rap. Knock, knock, knock.

Louise's special knock made her heart thump. Was this truly the last time she would open the door to her best friend?

"Louise Conrad, don't you make me cry already," Emilie whispered fiercely when she saw her friend's puckered eyebrows and wobbly chin.

"I'm sorry," Louise quavered. "It's just that—oh, this is bad of me—I thought if Karl refused to go, your parents might change their minds."

Emilie swallowed. "But we're so happy he's agreed to come."

Louise nodded. "Mama warned me to rejoice with those who rejoice." She paused to give rejoicing a chance to break forth, but it didn't.

"This way is good for you, Lusey. This is your house now. You won't have to knock on this door ever again."

"I'd rather have you than your house," said Louise.

The girls stood still on either side of the door, mouths firmly closed, their blue eyes careful pools of tears. Emilie broke the spell by pushing the door farther open. Louise stepped inside.

"Frau Borner, I have *Apfelkuchen.*" Louise held an enamel pan out to Mama. "The trees aren't bearing very well, but the apples are tasty."

"It will be delicious, Louise." Mama smiled broadly as she accepted the apple dessert. "And only the early trees are bearing now. There'll be more apples later; you'll see."

Louise nodded. "Mama says it's a day to feast together, not to horde." At Louise's words, Emilie looked about the kitchen. The table held a basket of hard rolls, logs of Thuringer sausage, a few jars of dill pickles, a bit of liverwurst, a pan of gingerbread. It was not the feast they would once have had, with vats of potato salad and coleslaw, kettles of potato soup with dumplings, wienerwurst, four kinds of dessert, milk, wine, coffee with cream, and pieces of *Kandiszucker*—sugar candy— for the children. But still people came to the kitchen, laughing and talking, filling their plates, and moving outside to picnic.

"Emilie, go on, visit with your friend," said Mama. "The work is done."

Just as Emilie and Louise started for the table, Mama interrupted. "There is one more thing. Would you girls carefully slide the trunkful of china into the pantry? I'm afraid with all the people it will be kicked and bumped about."

Emilie and Louise grasped the handles of the china trunk and slid it across the plank floor into the pantry.

"This is a pretty trunk," Louise remarked, noting the swirls carved into its wooden lid. "But America letters say not to take china—or pots and pans, for that matter."

"We're not taking much more than the feather beds and clothing, like the letters say to do," Emilie answered. "But Mama insisted on the china, because Karl has to inherit it. Want to see it?"

Louise shrugged. Emilie unsnapped the latches and lifted the lid.

"It's called lusterware," Emilie explained, as the girls peeked through the wrappings at the glazed copper and blue

13

dishes. "See how the surface glows in the light? It almost makes rainbows." Emilie unwrapped the cream pitcher and tipped it back and forth in a sunbeam from the pantry window. "As the oldest child of his parents, Papa inherited these from my *Grossmama*, and Karl will inherit them too."

"They're pretty," Louise agreed, "but won't your mama scold?"

At that moment another voice did cry out, but it wasn't Mama's. "Emilie! My favorite Emilie! I'm going to sail all the way to America right next to you. Mama said I could." Emilie jumped and almost dropped the pitcher.

"Heidi!" she cried with delight, turning to the pantry doorway where six-year-old Heidi Jurgen stood beaming at her. Emilie slapped the cloth wrapping around the pitcher, placed it in the trunk, and lowered the lid, all the while smiling back at Heidi's gap-toothed grin. "I'm glad your mama said that." She sprang up, hugged the little girl, and ran a hand over Heidi's brown curls. "I will love going on the ship with you, *Liebchen*. You may eat with us now, if you like."

Emilie expected the girl to squeal in instant agreement, but she said, "I want Mama to fix my plate. I'll come find you later."

Once outside, Emilie and Louise saw how many people had come to the send-off. Groups of men, including Heidi and Erich's father, Reinhard Jurgen, stood sipping coffee, discussing politics or church matters. Others sat around tables, playing card games such as *Skat* or *Schafskopf*—sheepshead. Papa didn't object to cards as long as no one played for money.

Women spoke of food prices and of young people forbidden by law to marry unless they would emigrate. An ancient woman grasped the hands of Della Jurgen, Heidi's mother and Erich's stepmother, and began praying. Emilie studied the mountain of Frau Jurgen's belly, and guessed what the prayer was about.

Schoolmates and church friends began approaching, saying "Godspeed, Emilie," or "It was good to know you, Emilie." Touched that they cared, she felt a prickling behind her eyes. Otto handled good-byes by challenging each one to an arm wrestle, or by friendly pushing that only once progressed to rolling on the ground. Those who were tongue-tied stood at a distance and waved. Emilie waved back.

Her breath caught when she spied Wilhelm Klein staring at her, the top of his hair lifting in the breeze like a bird's wing. He wouldn't speak today either, she knew. Emilie held his gaze a long last time—five seconds, six—until Sophie Lenz broke free from the pack and embraced her, declaring she would miss Emilie forever and expected heaps of America letters. Emilie cried a little. But when she went back to eat under the shade tree with Louise, Emilie's tears dried right up.

"Emileee," came the silken voice.

Emilie didn't need to look up to know who this was, but she looked anyway. Her mouth fell open.

Rosamund Albrecht wasn't wearing the dark skirt with stripes around the hem that most of the women and girls wore. She was wearing a wine-colored dress with an eyelet collar and sleeves that puffed out above the elbow. Her blond hair was drawn into a topknot encircled by a narrow braid.

"This is how they do in America," Rosamund informed them. "Papa brought this dress back from Chicago, Illinois, and one for Mama, too."

Emilie found Rosamund's mother, Johanna Albrecht, at the center of an admiring crowd. Her dress looked much like Rosamund's, except it was emerald green. Rosamund's father, Lambert Albrecht, moved among the men with a smile and glad-hand, wearing a long black coat, vest, trousers, a choker, a black silk hat, and smoking an odorous cigar as thick as a bratwurst. Though everyone else was also dressed in Sunday best, the Albrechts always managed to look grander.

"Papa was rich even here, of course," Rosamund went on. "And being kin to Duke Ernest, was important at court. The duke so hated to see him go, but he understood. Papa's always been destined for greater things."

Emilie was speechless; Louise, too. Emilie quickly tired of

craning her neck to look at Rosamund, but she intended to stay in the cool shade and eat her dinner.

"Your papa and Karl should go first, instead of all of you going," Rosamund advised. "Of course, they would probably find farmland rather than settle in a cultural center like Chicago. Then Karl could stay behind and run things, like Hans and Dieter stayed in America running Papa's business, and your papa could come back for you. You might be ready in, say, two years or so."

Emilie swallowed a lump of Thuringer whole.

"Do sit with us, Rosamund," Louise purred, wriggling closer to the tree trunk to make space in the shade. "Or would you stain your dress? Maybe in America the women stand all the time?"

Rosamund scowled. "Is that your latest rumor, you little gossip? I'm here to talk to Emilie. The least I can do, with the experience we've had, is offer direction."

Emilie's temper boiled over. Experience? When had Rosamund traveled more than fifty German miles out of the duchy? "The only direction I want from you, Rosamund Albrecht," she seethed, "is to go east when I am west, back when I am forth, up when I am down. And since I am now down and you are up, I do not invite you to sit. Go stand someplace else."

Rosamund's face bloomed red. "You bet I will stand. I'll stand on the ship's deck in the warm sunshine and salt-sea air, but when the storms come, I'll also stand in my cabin, which will be tall enough to stand *in*. You will lie in your miserable berth in steerage with your lice-ridden bunk mate, where you will not even be able to sit without cracking your head, breathing the stink of 200 bodies who haven't felt a breeze in four days." Rosamund turned on her heel.

"That shows how much you know," Emilie shouted, attracting the attention of most everyone in the yard. "We're not going in steerage. Our tickets are for cabin berths."

Rosamund glanced back with a thin smile. "Then it looks like we'll both be up, doesn't it?" She shrugged. "Guess you can't win."

Mama appeared at Emilie's side, drawing her behind the tree. "What has gotten into you, shouting so rudely in front of everyone we know? Is this how you want them to remember you, boasting about a cabin berth?"

"I'm sorry, Mama. But Rosamund started—" Emilie tried again. "She was being so hateful—"

"Someone else's bad behavior is no excuse for your own."

"I'm sorry, Mama."

Despite this rough spot, most of the afternoon passed in a stream of merrymaking. Voices buzzed, laughter erupted, mouth organs wheezed, people danced. Heidi Jurgen tugged at Emilie's hands, begging her and Louise to lead the younger children in the *Vogelsong*.

"Ready?" Emilie asked the six youngsters Heidi had gathered. "Here we go!" Bravely, she began to sing: "*Kommt ein Vogel geflogen ...*"

She breathed a sigh of relief as Louise and the children joined in, acting out the favorite song about a bird who comes flying, bringing a message from Mama. They fluttered their arms and blew noisy kisses when they sang, "Fly back with a greeting for Mama and a kiss," and smiled satisfied smiles at the last lines, "But I cannot come to her, I must stay here."

How sweet the little ones are, Emilie thought, enjoying their huge, bright eyes. Suddenly her own filled with tears. Tomorrow, would she really leave them all behind?

From then on, the celebration seemed to dissolve in a flood of weeping. Women sobbed over Mama, fretted over how near Della Jurgen was to giving birth, and wailed over who would next uproot themselves to risk their lives at sea and in a strange country. Otto gave up wrestling. Men twitched their mustaches. Karl and Erich grew somber, too, observing the throng and exchanging hushed words.

"How can it be we'll never see you again?" voices lamented.

"I'm glad for your prayers, but please don't worry," Della Jurgen soothed a friend. "God is my strength and my shield."

Even Johanna Albrecht was crying, but her husband was not. Still shaking hands and slapping shoulders, he worked the crowd, cigar bobbing at the corner of his mouth, heartily assuring everyone they hadn't seen the last of Lambert Albrecht. Rosamund was nowhere to be found.

"I'm not sure I can stand this much longer," Louise told Emilie. "Do you want to go walking?"

Emilie felt a pang of dread. A private parting with Louise would be harder to bear than this scene, but she couldn't refuse.

"Over here," said Louise, "under these trees near the house." When they'd sat down, Louise pulled a pair of sewing shears from her skirt pocket and tipped her head to one side. Her long, dark-blond hair fell in front of her shoulder.

With one clean snip she laid on her knee a four-inch lock of hair. Pulling a tie from the back of her head, a calico cord made from a strip of apron, she fastened it around the lock. This she presented to Emilie.

Wordlessly, Emilie did the same, and within a minute Louise was holding a lock of brown hair, bound in a plaid tie.

"You have to come back," Louise said, eyes brimming. "It's not like going into eternity. I'm sorry I said that. People go back and forth all the time now. You have to come back and see me."

"Or you can come over, when you're older." Emilie gulped. "I'll sponsor you. I'll meet your boat."

"Well, just don't pass up any chances to come back and show us how fine you are," Louise insisted. "I don't want the first person I see from America to be old Rosamund."

Both girls gave a sudden, spluttery laugh. They tucked the locks of hair into their skirt pockets and got up, but as they reached the kitchen in search of dessert, their cheeks were streaming. Near the door to the pantry, making eyes at Karl and Erich Jurgen, stood Rosamund.

The young men used the girls' entrance as their chance to escape, and Rosamund clucked her tongue at Emilie and Louise. "Are you carrying on too, like everyone out there? Have they got you believing you won't see each other for all time? How backward! It's disgusting."

"Rosamund." Emilie wiped her eyes. "If you have no one you're going to miss, I feel sorry for you."

"Well!" Rosamund huffed.

Louise elbowed Emilie. "Now do you see why you have to visit me?" Breaking into melodrama, Louise fell on Emilie's shoulder. "Oh, friend, have mercy. She's coming back! She's coming back!"

Helpless, Emilie and Louise burst into giggles.

"Of all the revolting, immature . . ." Rosamund stamped out of the house. This brought on another attack of laughter. Holding their sides, the friends headed past the pantry toward the last bits of *Apfelkuchen* on the table. But Emilie stopped still. Something wasn't right in the pantry.

"Look, Lusey." Emilie went into the pantry, Louise following. "We didn't leave the trunk standing crooked like this."

"It was Rosamund!" Louise declared. "She's just the kind who would snoop to see if your dishes were as good as theirs."

"We don't know that for sure," Emilie murmured, but she too found it easy to believe that Rosamund would root around in the trunk. The girls knelt on the floor and Emilie lifted the lid.

She was surprised, and somehow a twinge disappointed, to find the dishes in order. All the pieces were as tightly and smoothly wrapped as Mama had packed them, except for the cream pitcher, which was loosely swathed in a square of blanket the way she herself had left it.

"We'd better just latch this and leave it alone," Emilie said. "There's burlap on that shelf. Can you reach it, Louise? I think there's newspaper near the stove, too. Let's just pack it over the top of everything, for good measure."

Emilie settled the cream pitcher more snugly among the dishes. She layered burlap and newspaper over the top for extra padding. Then the girls lowered the lid, fastened the latches, eased the trunk straight against the wall, and left the pantry.

The dishes were packed. The clothes, nonperishable food, family Bible, best linens, hand tools, needles, and thread—all were packed. As the sun went down on the last Sunday in August, as Emilie hugged Louise in a last good-bye, she marveled that tomorrow she would begin making her way out of Germany, soon to set sail into that setting sun. The time to leave for America had come.

Chapter Three

When Emilie rose at dawn on Monday, she didn't have to milk the cow, shovel manure, or work in the fields. Instead, she loaded her bundles into a waiting wagon.

Church friends had kindly offered to transport the three families to the town of Minden, where they would board a steamboat to the port of Bremen. Once Karl had arranged to ride with the Jurgens, and Heidi with the Borners, the wagons began to roll. Emilie and Heidi sat tightly together, hands clasped.

"Are you sad, my favorite Emilie?" Heidi asked. "Don't be sad. Everybody's all together."

Emilie studied Heidi's eager, earnest face. "You mean Erich, don't you? And Karl." Feeling both sad and excited, Emilie decided to concentrate on being excited. "You're right, Heidi. If our families are together, that's the most important thing."

"I praised and praised and praised the Lord when Erich told Papa he'd come," Heidi declared. "I said thank You, Lord, thank You, Lord, thank You, Lord."

Emilie sat silently for a few minutes. When she was six, she hadn't felt tied to this place, either. Anywhere Mama and Papa had gone would have been good enough for her. Little ones understood such simple, clear truths sometimes. No wonder Jesus said we should enter His kingdom like a child.

The sun rose higher, and the day grew hot. Emilie began to sweat, even though her thick hair was braided to keep it off her neck. As the wagons bounced over ruts, Otto announced, "Now you'll see why riding in the last wagon is best." He squeezed one eye closed, took aim, and flung a stone into the road behind them.

"Otto, what is this?" questioned Mama. Emilie saw that his cupped hand brimmed with pebbles.

"Hit the hole, ten points." Otto pitched another stone. "Come close, five points. If it rolls off the road, minus five."

"I suppose you're the one who decides what is close," Emilie said.

"All of them." He chucked another. "Twenty points already!"

"*Wunderbar!*" Emilie snatched a portion of stones from her astonished brother. "My score shall be a sight to behold." To her delight, the wagon hit a sizable hole at that moment. Ready, aim, fire, in a nice, smooth arc at the retreating hole. "Score!"

Since there was no one following who could be hit by the stones, Mama let the game continue. Emilie caught sight of Rosamund Albrecht in the wagon ahead, looking back with disdain. She didn't care. She shared her stones with Heidi, and by the time they were gone and Otto had won, several more miles had passed behind them.

Night fell as they rolled through the Weser hills and past Teutoburg Forest, stopping at every border to pay duty. It was near midnight when the travelers finally crawled out of the wagons in Minden, stiff and weary.

"I've never stayed up this late before," Heidi reported. She'd been dozing, but there was still a hint of triumph in her voice.

"Not even my papa stays up this late," Emilie replied.

Papa shepherded his family to a door. "This is the inn Agent Langemann arranged for us. He promised the place would be decent."

"What's *decent?*" whispered Heidi.

"Good enough," Emilie replied, but later, drifting off to sleep, she changed her mind. Decent was lamplight to greet you, the salt tang of gravy on biscuits, crisp sheets smelling of soap. Decent could be more than just good enough. Decent was sometimes the very blessing of God.

*   *   *

After a morning passport check, Emilie's group joined a

crowd boarding the steamboat for the half-day trip to
Bremen. The weather continued warm and sunny. Pure white
clouds floated above smoke from the boat's stack. A breeze
ruffled colored triangles of bunting strung between four flag-
poles from bow to stern.

Emilie enjoyed looking over the side of the boat, smelling
the scent of water, and hearing its sloshing as the side-wheels
circled forward, ever forward.

"Do you suppose America will look like Germany?" an
older girl named Brigitte asked Emilie as they watched the
winding river.

"I hear America is so big it's completely different in different places," she answered. "Where are you going?"

"New York."

Emilie shook her head. "I don't know about New York,
except we will land there. We're going to Wisconsin, where
they say it is very much like here."

"I've talked to others on the boat," Brigitte replied. "Some
have no idea where they're going or what they will do when
they land."

"Are they emigrating for adventure?"

"One or two. Young men, for certain. But some didn't want to
leave. Their towns paid to send them away. No jobs, no skills." The
girl lowered her voice. "Some are women with children and no
husband. No prospects in Germany for mama or baby."

Emilie didn't know what to say.

"You know about that, don't you? How they will not let
people marry unless they have land or a job? So then, oops,
the babies come. What good does their rule do?"

Uneasily, Emilie sneaked a peek at Brigitte's middle.

"I'm not talking about myself!" Brigitte flared. "I know
where I'm bound, remember? New York!"

"I'm sorry," Emilie said, shaken.

"My sister, though." Brigitte calmed herself. "She is having
to leave her Anton. She is not *schwanger*, mind you, no babies

without marriage for her. But she goes, he stays, and everything is *kaputt* between them."

"I'm sorry," Emilie repeated. "Mama says the Bible teaches that people should be allowed to marry."

After meeting Brigitte, Emilie felt more solemn about this steamboat that carried different people, to different futures, for different reasons. She began to pray, strolling the deck, asking God to guide those who needed a place to go, to show Brigitte's sister a good life in America. She prayed for Otto, her towheaded, floppy-haired brother who thought himself funny, and for Karl, with his steely jaw and eyes and big dreams.

* * *

The sun was headed down the sky once again when they reached the seaport of Bremen. Heidi Jurgen held Emilie's hand, exclaiming, "Boats, boats, boats! Look, my favorite Emilie. These must be all the boats in the whole world!"

"But they aren't," Emilie told the little girl fondly. "There are many other boats in other cities by the sea."

"Let's get on that one." Heidi pointed.

Emilie thought Heidi meant the ship with a mermaid statue on its prow, but in truth she couldn't tell. Ships of all nations crowded the harbor, with flags of every color waving high and free. Carved figures of animals and mythical creatures graced their bows, and a forest of masts held countless white sails waiting to billow in the wind. Emilie caught some of the ships' names—*Electra*, *Mimi*—but the jostling mass of people blocked her view. Suddenly concerned that she might lose her family, Emilie turned and fixed her eyes on Mama's back.

"This way." She steered Heidi.

"But I want to get on the ship with the lady fish. Tell my papa we want that one."

"*Liebchen*, that one might not even be going to America," Emilie explained. "Maybe to England or somewhere else. And our ship doesn't sail till Thursday."

"When's Thursday?"

"We're staying at an inn here for two nights. Agent Langemann arranged our lodging."

Emilie looked for Mama again. Mama's red-brown dress, and the fringed shawl around her shoulders, were farther ahead now.

"You are lost, *Fraulein?*"

Emilie turned sharply. A short man, respectably hatted, stepped out of the milling crowd to join them.

"If you're waiting to board ship, I'll gladly check your tickets and direct you to the proper place." The man's reddish mustache stretched above his teeth as he smiled.

"Please, sir, I like the lady fish boat," requested Heidi.

"No! No, thank you," Emilie said quickly. She took a breath to calm herself. "My papa has our tickets."

"And where is your papa, exactly?" The man surveyed the multitude, as if he might know Papa if he saw him.

"Finding our lodging," Emilie said firmly. "Agent Langemann has taken care of everything."

At this, the man's gray eyes lighted up. "Agent Langemann! Why, Walter Langemann and I are the closest of associates. I'm pleased to assist his customers, as he is to assist mine. Schmidt is the name." The man tipped his hat. "Johann Schmidt."

Emilie nodded uncertainly.

"Take me to your father," Herr Schmidt suggested. "I'll examine his lodging reservations and escort you right to the door of the establishment. Walter and I use all the same emigrant housing for our clients."

Emilie wavered. The man knew Agent Langemann's given name, and had told her his own. Besides, in this throng of people she couldn't see her family at all anymore. If she failed to find them, it would be good to be in the company of Agent Langemann's colleague.

"I think this way—" she began.

"Emilie!" Out of nowhere, Karl grasped her right arm; Heidi was still attached to her left. "You piece of vermin," Karl yelled at Herr Schmidt, his blue eyes almost shooting sparks. Several people flinched and wriggled away from Herr Schmidt, leaving him a bewildered island in a sea of humanity.

"Maybe I managed to warn off a few more people," Karl muttered, as he steered the girls through the crowd.

"Is he a bad man, then?" Emilie asked, trying to match Karl's stride. "How did you know?"

"His kind crawl all over these seaports. Runners, they're called, and you can be sure they'll be waiting in America, too. They steal your ship passage and run. They tear up your inn reservations and lead you to some smelly flophouse, where the innkeeper charges you sky-high and pays the runner a fee. They offer to change your money for American dollars and then cheat you. Or just plain steal it all."

But Emilie hardly heard Karl once he mentioned America. "Why would they be waiting in America? Surely in America no one needs to rob?"

Karl swung in front of her and planted his hands on her shoulders. His blue eyes burned, but they were caring, not mean.

"I've talked to people. People here, and people who've come back from America."

"Like Herr Albrecht?"

"No, Emilie, listen. Like people who come back to stay."

Emilie was thunderstruck.

"Oh, yes. Many return. That's part of the reason so many leave illegally. They don't want to renounce German citizenship, in case they want to come back."

Emilie stared.

"Some come back because they went broke in America. And some went broke because runners met their ship and stole them blind. I heard of one who gave all his money to a man who offered to sell him Wisconsin farmland on the spot! Emilie, you've got to be careful every minute, especially of strangers. Promise me."

Emilie nodded. "I promise."

"I hear America sings of itself, it is the land of the free and the home of the brave," Karl said. "Maybe it's so. But you can be sure it's not the land without sin."

* * *

At Bremen's White Horse Inn, Emilie bathed with a cake of soap in a porcelain tub. Still dreaming of lolling in the water, of the slow drops plinking off her fingers, she woke on Wednesday, August 29, knowing this would be a day of waiting for departure. Such idleness was a new, odd feeling.

The weather was clear, and Emilie and Heidi got permission to go see the ships. "Look, Heidi, a ship is leaving!" Emilie exclaimed. She boosted the little girl to her shoulders to watch a three-masted ship slide toward the Weser's mouth and the open sea. Above the drone of the crowd, Emilie could hear the snap of rippling flags.

"You mustn't let go of my hand for an instant," Emilie instructed, setting Heidi down. She tried to worm her way closer to the ships, but was bumped by bundles and bodies. Her feet were trampled by wooden slippers. Many of those flags and figureheads had surely been in the same places yesterday. Why were those ships still here?

"What's the name of our ship?" Heidi pumped Emilie's arm.

"The *Velma*, Papa said. I wonder if it's here." Emilie craned her neck, to no avail.

"Nope, no *Velma*," came a boy's nasal voice from their left.

Emilie turned. The boy wore a flat, billed cap, and looked to be about fourteen. "If you are a runner," she cried, alarming several people, "be off with you!"

To her frustration, the boy snorted with laughter. "What a greenhorn you are. I'm an emigrant, same as you." He squinted at her. "You haven't been waiting half long enough, though. You're too clean."

Emilie had noticed the boy smelled ripe. In fact, so did much of the crowd.

"Haven't got half an inkling what I mean, have you?" The boy shook his head. "I was supposed to sail last Friday, but no sign of the *Admiral Finch*. Thousands of these people are in the same fix. Word is, ships aren't budging. Unfavorable winds."

"But a ship just left! These are packet ships; they sail on schedule. And it's very windy today," objected Emilie.

"Well," the boy said. "You can't have just any wind. It's got to blow the right way. Anyway, I've had all day and all night to watch the ships, and there's no *Velma* in port. Nope. No *Velma* at all."

"What do you mean—all day and all night?"

"You don't think I pay to sleep in that rathole they call housing, do you? Nope. Out here's good enough for me."

Emilie's heart sank. Obviously, this boy's trip wasn't planned by Agent Langemann. She hoped it hadn't been planned by Johann Schmidt. "I will say a prayer for you," she told him. He shrugged. "I will ask that the—*Admiral Finch*—will be in port tomorrow."

*   *   *

Emilie lay awake in her narrow cot that night, long after Mama, Heidi, and even Frau Jurgen had finally dropped off to sleep. Just as she was thinking she might be the only one awake in the entire inn, she heard hushed voices in the hall.

"I found it, Karl, right in the harbor, easy as water."

Otto! What was he doing up?

"Is that so, smart guy?" Karl chuckled fondly.

"Of course, most of the crowds are back at the emigrant houses by now. Perfect stink holes, some of those places!"

Thinking of the boy at the pier, Emilie shuddered.

"And a lot of the ships sailed today," Otto said. "Even a big lummox like you could've slipped in and out and around."

"So it's there in the harbor? The *Velma*?"

"Saw her with my own two eyes."

Emilie's heart leaped. Their ship was in Bremen! Waiting!

"Good," Karl said softly. "That's good."

Emilie threw back her sheet. She would have joined them, but the voices faded away and a key clicked in the lock. The door of her room eased open.

Chapter Four

"Karl!" Emilie cried softly. A flickering stub of candle lighted his face.

"Emilie?" Karl whispered. "What are you doing up?"

"What are you doing here?" she countered.

"Well, I—I'm bringing your key." The key made a muffled tap as Karl set it on a table. "Somehow I got hold of it, but it should be with you."

"Why did you send Otto out looking for the *Velma?*"

Karl froze. "I might have known you heard that, too."

"We'll talk in the hall." Emilie, in her white nightdress, crept carefully out of bed. "We can't wake Heidi's mama."

"There's nothing to talk about," Karl protested, but Emilie slipped past him and out the door. Karl and his candle followed. "I only wanted to know if the ship had come." Karl closed the door behind them. "Now we can rejoice and sleep soundly, instead of lying awake wondering if we sail tomorrow. Agreed?"

"Oh, I'm thrilled it has come," Emilie said. "Did Otto remember any other names of ships? Did he see the—*Admiral Finch*, maybe?"

Karl frowned. "The *Admiral Finch?*" Understanding came into his eyes. "You talked to someone today."

"Just a boy! He's going to America, like us, but he was supposed to leave almost a week ago. Did Otto see him sleeping near the pier?" she asked worriedly.

"Among all the others out there, you mean?" Karl whispered intensely. "Emilie." He brushed hair from her face with the back of his hand. "I don't mean you should never be kind

29

to people. I know you have a good heart. But please, be careful." Again, his blue eyes flamed.

She returned his gaze. "I can't promise to keep always to myself. But I promised I'd be careful, and I will."

Karl took a step back. "Good. That's good, then."

"I'll see you in the morning."

Karl smiled. "You're seeing me in the morning right now."

Emilie giggled. "Goodnight, Karl."

"Goodnight, Emilie."

She watched him walk down the hall, the light from his candle bobbing oddly along walls and doors. Before disappearing into his room, he turned to look at her one last time.

*   *   *

Thursday morning, too, the sun smiled on them. The entire party was at the dock bright and early to board ship. "Do we have everybody?" Papa asked.

The Albrechts were there: Lambert, Johanna, and Rosamund. The five Jurgens were assembled: Reinhard, Della and the child she carried, Erich, Heidi. The Borners were ready too, but Emilie, dressed in her best skirt and white blouse, could see only four members of her family.

"Where is that son of mine?" Papa wondered, glancing among the rambling people. His tone wasn't angry, but it was businesslike.

Rosamund sidled close to Emilie. "Be sure not to get your ticket out until it's asked for," she cautioned.

"I wouldn't," Emilie said coolly.

"You needn't be so uppity, as if you're somebody. I'm just trying to help."

"Where is he?" Papa said louder.

"Help comes from a friend," Emilie told Rosamund. "Not from someone who thinks *she* is somebody."

"Lord of all comfort, unite us . . ." Papa prayed.

"A lot you know," Rosamund murmured. "Duke Ernest, my papa's kin, helps thousands, and he is the biggest somebody of all."

"Rosamund," said Emilie, "you do realize that where we're going, everyone is equal? I somehow think you won't like America much at all."

"Thank You, God," breathed Papa.

Emilie turned from Rosamund, in the direction Papa was looking. "Otto!" she cried, as her younger brother appeared, shaking white-blond hair from his eyes. "Hurry up, *kleine Druckser.*"

"Who are you calling slowpoke?" Otto protested. "I can cover this wharf in a quarter of an hour."

"Stay here now," Papa said shortly. "Karl, we're to carry our baggage this way."

Karl lifted a duffel to his shoulder and picked up a suitcase. As the entire group snaked forward, it seemed to Emilie that they were actually joining a line. Her heart leaped.

Or maybe she was wrong about a line. Emilie had trouble keeping her eyes on Mama's back as they forged ahead. Too many people were dressed alike. She concentrated on Frau Jurgen's swaying form and on Heidi dancing along beside her. She watched the tall, black hat of Herr Albrecht, and even found her eyes glued to Rosamund's braided hair. The group gathered more or less in a huddle again, near a booth of some kind, their trunks about their feet.

"I believe we get our tickets checked here, stamped or such," Papa said. "Right, Lambert?" Emilie didn't quite follow their exchange, but learned that Papa was largely correct.

"Now where's Karl?" asked Mama. Everyone glanced around.

"Why, where's Erich?" echoed Della Jurgen. Her rosy cheeks flamed.

The entire party turned, leaned sideways, peered between shoulders or crooks of elbows, and stood on tiptoe. Nobody caught even a glimpse of Erich or Karl.

Papa stooped to the pile of luggage, lifting handles and letting the bags thump down again. Herr Jurgen joined him. They straightened, wearing grim faces.

"They've taken off," Papa said. "Their satchels are gone."

"What?" cried Mama. "*Ach*, they can't do that. How could they?"

"By plan, I suspect." Papa's face suddenly looked old. "Karl was stirring most of the night." He turned sternly to Otto. "As were you. Do you know anything about this?"

"No, Papa." Seeing Otto's shock and wide eyes, Emilie felt sure he was telling the truth. "Karl only asked me to sneak here and look for the *Velma*."

"He gave no reason for this?" Papa said impatiently.

"He said . . ." Grimacing, Otto seemed to run out of words.

"He said," Emilie continued, drawing all eyes to herself, "he was checking to see if the ship had come, so we could rest at ease about sailing today."

"Emilie? When did you speak to Karl? You were up in the night?" Mama asked.

"I heard Karl and Otto in the hall. I made Karl tell me what he was doing."

"That's all?" Mama pleaded. "That's all he said? Try to remember."

"He said," Emilie repeated, heart sinking, "I should be careful."

"He said when I'm an American, I shouldn't forget where I came from," Otto put in.

"In other words," Papa said slowly, "he told you good-bye."

"No," Mama moaned. She moaned again. "He did not tell *us* good-bye."

"And risk we'd catch on? He couldn't. He didn't mean to hurt you, Meta," Papa soothed.

"How could he be so cruel," Mama sobbed, "to go with us almost to the boat itself and then desert us? The son I know is not cruel like this."

"Not cruel, no," Papa said. "Just absorbed with himself. I understand now. He pretended he'd emigrate, searched out the ship last night, came this far today to make sure we sail. Had we missed Karl and Erich any sooner, we wouldn't leave. He knew that."

"And being so smooth with words, what did your master-mind of a son tell mine, do you suppose?" thundered Reinhard Jurgen. Emilie stared at the man, mustache quivering in his anger. "Where did he persuade him to run?" Frau Jurgen, hand atop her belly, held her husband's arm and peered at him, concerned.

Heidi Jurgen burst into sobs. Emilie cried, "Nowhere!"

All eyes jumped to her again, sharply this time.

"That is, I—I'm sorry." She took a breath. "Herr Jurgen, I think I can answer your question."

"Speak up, daughter," Papa commanded quietly.

"Once I heard Karl and Erich talking behind the barn," Emilie said. "Neither one tried to persuade the other. They agreed to go to university. They wanted to join the—"

"Join the what?" Reinhard Jurgen's growl was not unkind.

But Emilie had no hope of remembering the long name. "I don't know," she fretted. "A political group, I think."

Her papa and Heidi's exchanged serious glances. The Albrechts studied the two families as if they couldn't believe the rabble they had to travel with.

"What university?" Mama asked softly. Her pale blue eyes were now absolutely dry. "Did they name a city? Think, *Liebchen.*"

Emilie did. *Oh, Louise, I miss you already,* she thought. *You're the only other person who heard the places they mentioned.* But the names came clearly to her. "Heidelberg. Göttingen." There was a third one, one near home. "Jena."

"Jena." The word seemed to rumble up from deep inside Papa.

"Franz," Mama met Papa's eyes, "I must go after him."

Papa shook his head. "Meta, he's not twenty-one, but he's old enough to look after himself. We're ready to board ship."

"And we really must show our tickets, get the luggage on," Lambert Albrecht asserted, checking his pocket watch.

Indeed, Emilie vaguely heard a bell chiming, a voice booming about boarding for the *Velma*, but she was too agitated to listen. "Mama! What do you mean? You've got to come!"

Mama put her hands on Emilie's shoulders. Mother and daughter were very nearly the same height. "Emilie, I have to do this. I would do the same for you, or for Otto. Someday when you're a mother, you'll understand."

"Meta," said Papa.

"You are a good girl, a big girl. Responsible," Mama said. "You can take care of things in America, I know it."

Take care of things? Panic flooded Emilie. "No, no, no." She could think of nothing but this word. "No."

"Yes, Emilie," Mama whispered. "God will go with us both."

Emilie wanted to scream no a million more times, but staring at Mama, suddenly realized how it would crush her. She tightened her mouth. Sorrow began leaking from her eyes.

"What is it with this man . . . can't handle his own wife," Emilie heard Herr Albrecht mutter.

"Franz." Mama left Emilie now and went to Papa. "If we all leave on this ship, Karl will be lost to us. He will feel we're on one side of the ocean, while he is on the other, and a separation will grow that might never be overcome." She paused. "And he may wander farther from God than he already has."

"Can you prevent that separation?" Papa asked. "He will believe we have all left, whether or not it's true."

"But he will soon know I haven't gone," Mama returned. "Because I will find him."

Rosamund appeared at Emilie's elbow. "You'll want to hurry and get on ship," she buzzed, "unless you want the worst berth in the worst cabin."

"Rosamund, *halte den*," Emilie snapped. Rosamund gasped, but she did indeed shut up.

Papa had still not answered Mama. Then, slowly he spoke. "We will write to you in care of Ernst Conrad, as soon as we land."

Emilie closed her eyes. Sweat trickled under her blouse; the sun's heat pressed on her head. Her mama was not going to America. Would she faint here on the dock?

Mama turned to the Jurgens. "I will find them both. Have faith, and go on to America. You need each other. I will find them both."

Reinhard Jurgen's anger had dissolved. Frau Jurgen peered at her husband, then nodded thanks to Mama with a tiny, sad smile.

Heidi sobbed as if her heart would break.

Mama found her own valise and picked it up. Emilie knew Mama also had money pinned inside a pocket, as did she. Because of pickpockets, Papa had thought it wise that all their funds not be carried by one person. Emilie wondered if the pocket money that allowed Mama to follow Karl had also enabled Karl to leave in the first place.

Mama made no move to go, and the Jurgens drew closer. "We cannot part without prayer," Papa said.

"Did you people wish to sail today?" Lambert Albrecht's big-hearted manner was fading fast. "The ship is loading!"

"Will you join us in prayer?" Papa called to him.

"After you failed to control that son of yours, now you would pray about it?" Albrecht muttered. He waved his hand in dismissal.

"Then if you would be kind enough to see that our trunks get on the ship," Papa said. He bowed his head. "O gracious God, watch over our son and brother in his wanderings . . ."

"If your luggage leaves without you, I'll not be responsible," threatened Herr Albrecht.

". . . and guard his faithful mother, who in love has set aside herself . . ."

"Boarding . . ." chanted the announcer.

"And forgive us our sins . . ." prayed Reinhard Jurgen.

Clannggg, rang the ship's bell.

"Jesus, Jesus," sobbed Heidi Jurgen.

"The *Velma* ..."

"... and go with us, Lord Almighty; we depend on You as never before ..."

Clannggg.

"... in Christ's name we pray ..."

"Departure ..."

"Amen," chimed in Emilie.

Never minding the public show, Mama hugged and kissed everyone, Papa last. Then, gripping her valise, she said, "Go on, now. Get on the ship. Go on!" She spun and hurried through the crowd.

Emilie stared after her.

"Emilie." Papa turned her to him. "Your ticket." He thrust it into her hand. "This way. Go!"

But there were two tickets, she could feel, as she stumbled forward. Hers and Mama's, stuck together. She glanced at them. So many people would give anything to go to America, so many were weeping and wailing as they bid loved ones good-bye, so many had to stay behind and hope to be sent for someday. It was bad enough to waste Karl's passage, but Mama's, too? It was a shame. No, it was a sin.

She came upon a young couple, gripping hands. "I'll send money," implored the poor husband. "I'll save money, too, for your passage. Oh, pray God, it won't be long."

The wife only sobbed helplessly. Even as she hurried past, Emilie caught sight of the gentle roundness at the girl's waist. Though much farther from term than Della Jurgen, the young woman was pregnant.

Emilie halted. People bumped her, shouted, but still she backed up. "Here." Glancing one last time to make sure she held Mama's ticket, she thrust it between the pair's entwined fingers. "Cabin berth. Hurry."

"But ... what's this?" sputtered the bug-eyed couple.

"Your passage. Hurry." Emilie whirled forward again as the crowd blocked the two from her view.

"Are you an angel?" shrilled the man's tenor voice.

"Emilie?" Papa, waiting ahead, grasped her arm. "What were you doing, child?"

Emilie, not knowing what Papa had seen, did know she was spared an explanation for now. Praying that time had not run out, they could only join the surge toward the ship.

Chapter Five

After the swarm of thousands at the docks, the 500 people on the *Velma* seemed little more than a town-square gathering. To Emilie's surprise, though, the dashing around didn't stop.

"About one hundred are traveling in cabins," Papa told her and Otto on deck. "They are divided into two or three groups. Some of the bolder passengers have made a move to separate women from men, so we may be split up. We had better pick out our berths."

Emilie didn't understand. One hundred people, divided into two or three—cabins? Where was she supposed to go? But terse announcements from the ship's crew led her through a door into a room jammed with chattering women and girls. Bunks were lined up in two rows down the long walls. On all of them, it seemed, duffels and cloth bags and totes had been piled. Trunks scraped along the plank floor as their owners slid them under beds.

Emilie's heart sank. There was no room for her here. Or was there? The bunk next to the door was surrounded by people, but its thin mattress was bare. "Excuse me?" Emilie hardly heard herself squeak. She tried again. "Is this taken?"

A woman in a kerchief turned around. "If you want it, don't invite somebody else to grab it first."

"Emilie!" Startled, Emilie looked up to see Frau Jurgen wading forward. Relief flooded her. Removing Emilie's valise from her grasp, Frau Jurgen plunked it onto the empty bunk. "There." She smiled. "Your home for the next few weeks. Do you have other things you need help storing?"

"Well . . . I do have two trunks. One has—the rest of

Mama's things in it."

"Ahh," said Frau Jurgen.

"But it also has things we were advised to bring, like rope, needles and thread, tin cups and plates." She declined to mention the chamber pot.

"Very good."

"And the other trunk is the good china. We had to bring it because—" Emilie sighed, feeling both sad and silly about the useless things she carried. "Because Karl has to inherit it."

"Perfectly understandable," Frau Jurgen said softly. "Let's get settled in."

To Frau Jurgen's satisfaction, the china trunk slipped completely beneath Emilie's bed, while the other sat beside it. "This can be your table, of sorts," she said. "Now, I know a certain young lady who promised to wait quietly on her bunk until we called her."

"Oh, Heidi!" The thought of her small friend brought some cheer back to Emilie. "May I walk on the deck with her?"

The bitter voice that replied startled them both. "Sure. Go ahead." Rosamund stood in the aisle, regarding them haughtily. "But when you have to rub shoulders with what's out there, don't blame me. You dare tell your betters to shut up? Well, now you'll shift for yourself!"

"Thank heaven for that!" Emilie retorted. Frau Jurgen put a hand on her arm. Rosamund's green eyes narrowed to slits. She turned sharply and headed for a pair of berths in the far corner. Frau Albrecht, smoothing wrinkles out of several frocks, began fussing at her approach.

"Frau Jurgen," Emilie burst out, though she tried to speak low. "Why is Rosamund the way she is?"

The young woman sat on Emilie's bunk, close to the wall for privacy. "She's been trained to believe she is royalty," Frau Jurgen said.

Emilie nodded. That was really all the explanation she needed.

"But she is smart enough to notice when one of her 'inferiors' can match wits with her, is better loved, is happier," Frau Jurgen continued.

Emilie was amazed. "You don't mean—me?"

Frau Jurgen nodded.

"And I am happier?"

"Of course. Happy in your family, happy in your Lord. Rosamund doesn't have these things, and she is jealous. And being jealous of a—"

"Commoner?" Emilie supplied.

"Indeed." Heidi's mother laughed briefly. "Being jealous of a commoner makes her angry. Very angry." Frau Jurgen sobered. "The answer you gave her just now was deserved. But it was also proud, and it presumed that heaven was on your side. Do you know the Scripture, 'Pride goeth before destruction, and a haughty spirit before a fall'?"

Emilie nodded.

"Your pride will only increase Rosamund's anger against you. I don't want to falsely accuse her, but people who feel threatened can be tempted to seek revenge."

Emilie remained silent. Frau Jurgen was saying that Rosamund Albrecht could become an outright enemy.

"Rosamund, of course, falls under the Scripture's truth, too. Nobles, even real ones, aren't spared from downfall. The best thing you can do for Rosamund, and for your own attitude toward her, is to pray for her."

Emilie nodded. "I will, Frau Jurgen."

"And remember." Frau Jurgen took Emilie's chin gently in her fingers and looked her in the eye. "It's you who are a king's child. Whatever happens on this voyage, or in your new life, you are a king's child."

*   *   *

Emilie's cabin, occupied by eighteen females, felt less cramped as people finished settling in. With many then going out on deck, Emilie and Frau Jurgen walked easily up the aisle toward Heidi's bunk. Just as Emilie was marveling at the active girl's patience, she caught sight of Heidi huddled miserably against her pillow.

"Heidi!" Both her mother and Emilie hurried forward, but Frau Jurgen reached her first. Heidi's mother ran a hand over her forehead. "Are you ill?"

But they could see that her feverish look came from crying. "Jesus isn't real," the little girl whimpered. Emilie was stunned by her words. "Jesus isn't real."

Della Jurgen gathered her daughter close. "Oh, but He is, *Liebchen*, He is. You're thinking of Erich, aren't you? How we prayed and prayed for him to come with us, and he didn't."

"It didn't work," sobbed the child.

"Well, we won't stop praying," soothed her mother. "There, now, you're tired with all we've been through. Rest yourself." She spread a sheet over the child and Emilie tiptoed away.

Planning to go out on deck and perhaps find her family, Emilie was stopped again when she reached her own bunk. On the neighboring bed, surrounded by no luggage, sat the young woman to whom she'd given Mama's ticket.

"Hello!" Emilie greeted her. "You made it on board! I'm so glad. What's your name?"

The woman—girl, really—smiled strangely. "Well, I guess it's Meta Borner, isn't it?"

Emilie was flabbergasted. "Well, no. I'm sure you can use your right name on the ship."

"How do I know they don't throw off stowaways?" This was whispered so faintly that Emilie sat down on her bed, almost knee to knee with the girl.

"You're not a stowaway," Emilie said quietly. "You have a ticket for a cabin berth."

"Yes, issued in the name of Meta Borner." Though she was clearly nervous, a defiant sparkle touched the girl's brown eyes. "And I, as ticket holder, am Meta," she paused for effect, "Borner." She trembled fiercely.

"You're scared," Emilie consoled. "I don't think you need to be scared."

"I've heard stories," hissed 'Meta.' "The sailors hunt down those who don't belong. If they catch you soon enough, the ship turns back. But if they catch you on the open sea . . ."The woman shrugged meaningfully, and Emilie knew she was supposed to conclude that stowaways were tossed overboard.

"You feel guilty!" Emilie was shocked. "You aren't happy you accepted Mama's ticket!"

"I should never have let Jakob talk me into this. I wasn't ready to board a ship! But he was so convinced you were the blessing of God Himself."

Emilie's heart sank to her shoes. This young wife was angry at her husband, and at her!

"He is in steerage. I am here. How often will I see him? If I am put off the ship, will he even know? Or will they put him off, too?"

"You aren't making sense," Emilie said. "How would they know he's your husband if you don't give your right name? That is, if your stories are even true. And if the *Velma* is that kind of ship."

The woman shrank back, her brown eyes flashing in her pale face. "My name—is Meta."

She blames me that she's here, Emilie realized. The woman was scared, illogical, and likely to make a fuss if Emilie argued further. It was probably better to simply give in. "All right," she said. "Meta." She left the cabin.

On the main deck, sailors bustled about while passengers stood in confused groups. Emilie was dismayed to hear a crewman calling names from a ledger book. Could it be that the woman who had Mama's ticket really did need Mama's identity?

The people whose names were called made their way down a hatch. Below deck must be the place called steerage, and it sounded like the people were receiving some sort of assignment.

Emilie decided not to watch. Exhausted, grieved over Karl,

shocked by Mama's departure, she didn't even want Papa and Otto now. She wanted only to stop the churning in her soul.

She drew in a ragged breath, strolled to the rail near the bow, and looked out onto the water. A long spar, jutting from the front of the packet ship, held the foremost sails. Beyond this she saw a barge approaching the ship, sounding its bell. Sailors overran the *Velma*, pulling in lines that Emilie guessed had tethered the ship to the dock. As the barge took on these lines and began towing, the *Velma* slid forward.

People set up a cheer. Emilie, too, felt a small thrill in her heart. When the barge moved away, and the packet's sails unrolled and billowed in the wind, she left the rail and hurried toward the ship's stern.

Bremen lay behind, she knew, and whole villages of ships tucked into berths, with their webs of rigging and proud, colorful flags. Behind also lay two-fifths of her family. She had to glimpse one last time the place where they'd parted.

But as Emilie looked over the side, the ache in her throat faded. The barge that had hauled the *Velma* was taking on another packet, with its three masts and square sails. Her eyes widened. Lettered clearly in black near the bow of the ship, barely visible as the *Velma* pulled away, was the ship's name.

She knew no English, but she could sound out the first word: A-d-m-i-r-a-l. The second she thought was spelled funny—shouldn't it be F-i-n-s-c-h? But there was no doubt what ship this was. The *Admiral Finch* had come in!

Oh, Lord, You haven't forgotten me! Thank You for answering, for Christ's sake, and for that boy's sake, and for my sake.

"Ahh, my new friend," purred a voice, as a hand came down on her arm. The fingers could grip like steel if they chose; Emilie could feel it. "You asked my name, but I don't remember you offering yours."

She couldn't lie. Lying was wrong, and too many people on this ship knew her name. Didn't anyone besides 'Meta's' husband know *her* name?

"It wouldn't work for me to act as your mama, I suppose."
Meta giggled.

"You try it," Emilie huffed, "and I will tell my papa every-thing."

"I just told you it wouldn't work." Meta paused. "Your papa's on the ship?"

"Did you think I'd be all alone?"

"Well, you're not with your mama."

Emilie stared, appalled. "No, and you are with your hus-band at her expense!"

The young matron blanched. "Quick with your tongue, I see. Look, I didn't mean we should quarrel. I'm sorry."

Slightly mollified, Emilie nodded.

"But we're going to be neighbors in the cabin, and I need a name to call you."

She hesitated. "Emilie."

"Well, Emilie—I'm going to be needing a few things."

Chapter Six

For the next eight days, many passengers needed little except a place to be sick. Meta, wearing Mama's extra clothes despite her pregnancy, was among them. So was Emilie.

"Meta? You want zwieback?" Sprawled on her bunk, Emilie fished a piece of the crusty bread from the tin and poked it across the aisle.

"Don't even let me see it," groaned Meta.

Emilie had tired of telling Meta that dry bread might settle her stomach, that she needed something for her baby. She was so weak herself she almost dropped the zwieback on the floor. But she made herself plunk it back into the tin.

Meta slowly sat up. Thinking she planned to walk awhile, Emilie said, "I'm so dry. Would you bring me some water?" She rustled unsuccessfully on top of her trunk for her tin cup. She couldn't find anything anymore. Possessions were scattered hither and yon, with everyone too sick to care.

"Water?" Meta shuddered. "You want me to go near that stinking stuff in my condition? Go on with you." She sprang up, hand over her mouth, and lurched out of the cabin.

Emilie let her muscles sag and ran her tongue over her dry lips. How bad could the drinking water smell, compared to everything else on this ship?

The toilet rooms were overcome by a sour stench, even though the ship's crew cleaned them. The cabin, too, had grown fetid, the air close. Some people purposely retched right on deck, rather than foul an enclosed space. She recalled with embarrassment the time she herself had vomited over the side. The wind had caught gooey droplets and lashed them against her face and blouse. The mess itself, rather than disappearing into the sea, had splashed against the copper-plated hull, where it stuck.

"Emilie?" It was Frau Jurgen calling. "I've brought you some water. I'm going to insist you drink it, but slowly. You can't go on without this."

Emilie elbowed herself up and eased her legs over the side. Shakily, she bent double. "Thank you." She peered closely at Frau Jurgen, whose normally rosy cheeks had gone sallow. "Are you all right?"

Frau Jurgen smiled wanly. "No appetite, but getting along."

"And Heidi?"

"Better than most of us, praise God, though I did have to strip her bed in the night. The Albrechts almost had apoplexy."

Emilie snickered in spite of herself. "Maybe kin of Duke Ernest don't vomit."

Della Jurgen laughed too, but said quickly, "I shouldn't have made that remark. It was snide. Now here, take the water. Along with a little vinegar, I've added a teaspoon of honey."

Emilie sipped from the tin cup. "It's not bad. Would you help me fix a cup for Meta?" After eight days together in the cabin, Frau Jurgen had learned the story of Meta.

"Of course. I see you're taking good care of her."

"It's my fault she's on the ship with nothing. And I'm not the only one who looks out for her. Frau Bauer has been kind." Frau Bauer was the good but gruff woman who had advised Emilie to claim the open bunk. "But Meta is afraid of Frau Bauer."

Della Jurgen sighed. "Meta is afraid of much, it seems. I wonder what help she's getting from her husband?"

This struck Emilie as funny. She choked on her water. Dribbles flew. "But Frau Jurgen, after all, she cannot wear his trousers!"

For a split second she felt a pang of dismay. She hadn't intended to backtalk Heidi's mother. But Frau Jurgen, who seemed more like an older sister every minute, chuckled too.

Emilie drank two more cups of the treated water that day. She also persuaded Meta to have some. Her hopes, and even her strength, rose when they both kept the water down. Meeting with Papa and Otto on deck that afternoon, she saw that Papa was looking a bit gray. But Otto had gotten his sea legs early and all but swung from the packet's rigging.

After the three agreed to brave the dining hall that evening—armed with vinegar to dose the barley soup that would surely be served—Emilie excused herself to visit the privy. Mouth-breathing as she entered the busy room, she began to wonder if she could face supper after all. She set these thoughts aside, though, because while searching for an unoccupied toilet, she came upon Rosamund Albrecht.

Hidden in a corner, Rosamund was crying and pouring salt water down the front of her dress, swiping at it with a cloth. One whiff, one glance, were enough to tell Emilie the girl had thrown up on herself.

"Rosamund?" Emilie was afraid to interfere, but she couldn't turn her back. "If you want, I'll find your mama and tell her you need to change clothes." She remembered the abundance of dresses the two had brought.

"Emilie Borner, how dare you invade my privacy," Rosamund seethed. "Get out."

Emilie was too surprised to feel angry. Wouldn't anything soften Rosamund's heart? "But I'll help—"

"Go away!" shrieked Rosamund.

Hearing the tone that was far more desperate than irate, Emilie backed up hastily. Rosamund was embarrassed, she realized, by anything that made her come across as an ordinary human being. No wonder the girl had hardly been seen in days. She couldn't stand to be sick among the masses, and therefore be just like them.

As Rosamund lifted a large metal pitcher and drenched herself yet again, Emilie turned away. She told herself Frau Jurgen and Heidi were her friends, and Frau Bauer, and that even Meta wasn't a lost cause. And of course she had Papa and Otto. If Rosamund hated her—well, who could win them all?

She was on her way to supper when she realized her latest clash with Rosamund might increase the girl's malice against her.

* * *

After ten days on ship, almost everyone's seasickness had eased. That was the good news. The bad news was that the *Velma* had stopped pitching and rolling and creaking because the wind had stopped blowing. The packet was becalmed.

The main deck became crowded as people came up from steerage, to stroll and to stare at the miles of open water. Some beseeched God to fill the sails with the breath of life, but they remained limp. Emilie grew fascinated with the lines of people waiting to cook at the fireplace. "What are they doing?" she asked Papa.

"There's no dining hall in steerage," Papa replied. "They have to cook their own rations. Now that people feel well enough to eat, we'll probably see these long lines every day."

Emilie watched the line of steerage passengers. She spied a girl of nine or ten, who appeared to belong to none of the adults around her. She held a blackened frying pan containing a lump of fatty meat. That meat will spoil three times over before she gets to the head of the line, Emilie thought. She wanted to help, but what could she do? Besides, something about the girl's ramrod-straight figure warned Emilie not to show pity. She turned away.

The following day there was still no wind, and sitting idle began to frustrate the passengers. Emilie was unnerved by the stillness of the sea, and how it stretched to a sky so much the same color that she couldn't make out the horizon.

"I don't like feeling like a tiny speck in the middle of it all," confessed Frau Jurgen when Emilie shared her thoughts. "God knows where we are, but I declare no one else does."

Otto, who had pumped the sailors endlessly for sea stories

and worn out his welcome, was just plain bored.

Meta complained. Frau Bauer told her to buck up, that whining only piled affliction upon affliction. Rosamund and her mother sat neatly on their bunks, making needlepoint lace.

The behavior that distressed Emilie was Heidi's. She was amazed to have to coax the little girl into walking on deck, but when Heidi cowered at the sight of the ocean, Emilie was truly disturbed.

"It's scary." Heidi clutched Emilie around the middle so hard she gasped. "The world disappeared."

"Why, Heidi." Emilie knelt to see Heidi's face. "I think it's peculiar too, to see gray-blue-green everywhere we look. But we're just seeing a part of the world that's new to us."

"You're fooling," said Heidi. "Like when my papa says Jesus hears our prayers, and your papa reads his Bible to us, and my mama says the food isn't too awful and I should eat it. But it is! It stinks!"

"*Liebchen*, you've hardly eaten anything since we sailed. If I get you some prunes or dried apples, will you eat them?"

Wooden crates scraping across the deck drew their attention. Six men wearing blue jackets and hats and carrying black cases gathered around the crates. Snapping open their cases, the men unpacked shiny musical instruments. Lovely trills, high and low, filled the air as the musicians warmed up.

"Heidi, a band!" Emilie cried, delighted. "Do you know the names of the instruments?"

The child, sucking a finger, shook her head.

"Well, the skinny black one is a clarinet, the one that curves up at the bottom is a saxophone, the sliding one is a trombone. And the man in the middle has a concertina!" Emilie loved the little squeezebox that always promised lively dance music.

"What's the fat one?" Heidi asked dully.

In fact there were two instruments Emilie couldn't name. One looked like a small tuba, the other like a longer, thinner trumpet. "I don't know," she said.

Somehow she knew that was the wrong answer. Heidi said nothing.

Three of the men sat on the crates, the other three stood behind them, and with lively toe-tapping they struck up a tune.

It didn't take long for the area to fill with people, and for a great chattering to begin. Some passengers dropped out of the cooking line to dance. Emilie watched with interest as Meta and her husband whirled by.

"Meta's husband is a good dancer," she told Heidi.

"Now is your chance," Heidi replied.

Puzzled, Emilie stared at the child. "Chance for what?"

"To sneak close to them and hear her real name. Her husband will call her by it."

Emilie had never thought of this. Surprised that Heidi had, she was speechless.

"Then you can tell everybody who she is, and they can get her off the ship. She shouldn't be here. Your mama should. And if she was here, then Karl and Erich would be, too."

Emilie wrinkled her brow trying to sort out the little girl's logic. With a sinking heart, she realized she would disappoint Heidi again. "Please don't be mad at Meta, Heidi. She's on the ship because of me. So I have to help her, and I even want to. Can you understand?"

"*Nein!*" the child stormed. "She doesn't even say thank you!"

Emilie winced. This was so, and it had bothered her. But she realized Heidi couldn't understand. Back in Bremen, Emilie had thought she could hand someone Mama's ticket and walk away. It didn't work like that. There were responsibilities attached—and consequences.

Heidi's lip stuck out, and her eyes flooded. "Heidi, isn't the music pretty?" Emilie ran her hand lightly over Heidi's hair. "I'll dance with you, if you like. We can even do the *Vogelsong.*"

"*Nein!*" Heidi screamed again. "I'm going to find my mama!" She darted between the dancers and Emilie lost sight of her.

Emilie wasn't a sigher, but now bewilderment made her

sigh long and deep. Much as Heidi adored Erich, she should have bounced back by now. It wasn't happening.

"Emilie." The voice was familiar. Emilie turned. "I see Heidi isn't taking things very well," said Rosamund Albrecht.

Again, Emilie fell speechless. Rosamund was speaking to her? And not boastfully? She merely stood there, dressed modestly, blond hair braided sensibly, looking down at Emilie only because she was taller.

"Heidi doesn't believe what people say anymore, does she?" Rosamund continued. "Isn't that really what's wrong?"

Emilie found her voice. "I—think that's it, Rosamund. I think you're right."

"That's the trouble with religion, I think," said Rosamund. "You tell a child to say his prayers, and the prayers don't come true, and the child doesn't believe it's real anymore." She shrugged. "Then he wonders what else people lie about."

Emilie was astounded. She wanted badly to ask, "Is that how it is with you, Rosamund?" But Rosamund would likely bite her head off. She changed the subject. "Do you like the music?"

Rosamund spoke at the same time. "There are some people I want you to meet."

They actually laughed together.

"Of course I like the music," said Rosamund. "I'll teach you to dance."

"Oh, but I can," Emilie was growing eager. "The waltz, the *Schottische.*" She caught sight of her brother reeling along the floor, spoofing the dancers. "You know what we could do? We could teach Otto!"

Rosamund smiled pleasantly. "All right. Let's."

Amazed, Emilie cut herself off from showing it. "Otto! *Kleine Struwelpeter!*"

That brought him over. "Who are you calling 'shaggy-headed boy'?"

"You!" Emilie clucked over his floppy, white-blond hair. "We ought to pray there's a barber on the ship."

"Did you want something worthwhile?"

"Oh, indeed," giggled Emilie. "Rosamund and I have seen your pitiful attempts at dancing. We aim to teach you right."

Otto made popeyes and slid them over to Rosamund.

"Well?" prodded Emilie, beginning to bounce to the beat.

"Why should I learn to dance?"

"So you can dance with the ladies when you are a man," said Rosamund.

"Like Meta's husband," blurted Emilie.

Otto collapsed to the deck dramatically. When he got up, he said, "Who's Meta?"

"A girl." Emilie's stomach took a nervous swoop. "Come on, Otto, I need a partner. If you join me, I'll—I'll—buy you a kilogram of *Kandiszucker* in America."

The promise of candy did it. Otto dived into a dance and the three had a rousing good time, Rosamund laughing almost as much as Emilie at Otto's antics. *Maybe Rosamund hasn't made other friends on the* Velma, Emilie thought. The majority of emigrants were men, after all, and maybe Rosamund was just plain lonely.

Or maybe not. Hadn't Rosamund said she had someone for Emilie to meet?

Maybe the fact that she was dancing on a motionless ship on an empty sea with Rosamund Albrecht was just one of God's miracles.

Chapter Seven

Emilie's dancing slowed only when the music slowed and a girl began to sing.

Her voice was high, light, and clear. She stood on the band's left, and when the clarinet player offered her his crate, she shook her head. Emilie stared enchanted at the girl's straggly brown-blond hair and dark maroon dress. She recognized her. This was the girl with the frying pan from the steerage cooking line.

"I want to meet her," she said to Rosamund when the song ended. She almost asked Rosamund along, but was afraid Rosamund's friendliness wouldn't extend to a steerage girl. Rosamund made no move to go with her.

"Lotte Stein," the girl introduced herself.

"You have a beautiful voice," Emilie told her.

"*Danke schön.*" Lotte smiled shyly. "Mama hopes that in America I can have music lessons. In Germany, we were too poor."

"We had trouble too," Emilie said. "Bad crops. Is your mama here?" She looked around for a woman who might be Lotte's mother.

"Below. I'm afraid she's poorly."

"Seasick?"

Lotte nodded. "*Ja*, seasick, I'm sure that's all. She didn't want to come up, because our bunkmates did, and now she can stretch out in the berth. She needs the rest."

Emilie nodded, not quite sure what she'd just been told. "Come walking with me?"

The smaller girl's eyes lit up. "Really?"

53

"Well, sure." Emilie smiled. Lotte mustn't have had much attention from older girls before.

"You will make a good American," Lotte almost whispered as they headed away from the music.

Emilie laughed, surprised. "I hope to. But why do you say that?"

"You're practicing for when everyone is equal. Asking me to walk."

Emilie stared. Their walking slowed to a stop. "But we are equal. God loves us the same."

Lotte studied Emilie gravely, then flashed a small smile. "Maybe. After all, we're both going to America."

*   *   *

Three days later, on Thursday, September 13, Rosamund led her through a passageway Emilie hadn't known existed, toward the stern of the ship, to meet a passenger named Frau Blumenfeld. What she saw shocked her.

Frau Blumenfeld's cabin, warmly lighted by an overhead oil lamp, had a carpeted floor and dark, scrolled woodwork. A wardrobe of the same rich wood stood near a washbowl with a saltwater pump. Incredibly, perfume scented the air, filling Emilie with a sharp longing for the flower gardens of her childhood. The room held just two beds, one each for Herr and Frau Blumenfeld. Three copies of a magazine, the *Novellenzeitung*, lay at the foot of one. Emilie knew of it; the magazine published novels in serial form.

"Rosamund tells me you're good with children." Frau Blumenfeld smiled as she removed her dress hat. The hat was a straw-colored crescent worn with points to the sides, trimmed with large fabric balls, in black.

"The Blumenfelds have just returned from dinner with the captain," Rosamund supplied.

So that explained the woman's immaculate white blouse, her skirt the color of purple-red wine, her embroidered wine-and-black bodice. Frau Blumenfeld's hair was darker than even the Black Forest. She was exquisite.

"Actually, that was lunch in the dining room," Frau Blumenfeld amended, with another friendly smile.

Not in any dining room I've seen on this ship, Emilie thought. She realized there must be at least three classes of passengers on the *Velma*.

"So. You do like children?" the woman asked her again.

Emilie broke out of her trance. "Uh, yes, Frau Blumenfeld," she said brightly. "I love children."

"Wonderful." Frau Blumenfeld looked over her shoulder where a door—not the door to the corridor—stood ajar. "Elise! Stefan!"

The door swung inward and two children of five or six entered. Dressed almost as nicely as their mother, they quietly took their places in front of her. The silky-haired girl gazed at Emilie shyly through huge, brown eyes, while the little boy, with darker hair, freckles, and unbelievably long lashes, simpered.

"The children are accustomed to spending several hours a day with an attendant," Frau Blumenfeld said. "Playing games, doing lessons, reading stories—you do read, don't you, Emilie?"

Though growing more confused by the minute, Emilie replied quickly, "Oh, yes. I've always gone to school."

"Then, if you are interested, I see no reason not to offer you the position," the woman continued. "Rosamund has vouched for you, and if things aren't workable we'll discover that soon enough."

"Position?" said Emilie. She let her gaze flicker between Frau Blumenfeld and Rosamund.

Frau Blumenfeld's eyebrows shot up. "You didn't tell her, Rosamund?"

"Well," fawned Rosamund, "that is, I thought all of you should—meet, of course, before—anyone got their hopes up."

Emilie knew perfectly well that "anyone" meant her.

"Emilie, I apologize for being so presumptuous." Frau Blumenfeld looked straight at her now. "If you want the situation I've described, it's yours. We'll not go through an inter-view process just for a few weeks' ocean crossing. But if you're not a candidate for employment, I'll understand."

Emilie felt completely torn. Annoyed at Rosamund, she was nevertheless intrigued by the offer and the chance to earn money. She would love to read to Elise and Stefan. And what if—just what if, the children made good friends for Heidi? That alone might be reason enough to say yes.

"Frau Blumenfeld, I must ask my papa," said Emilie. "I will let you know as soon as he decides."

When the two girls left the Blumenfelds' suite, Rosamund caught up with her immediately. "Emilie. You aren't mad, are you?"

Emilie was. Obviously, Rosamund had recommended her to the Blumenfelds as someone of a lower class than they. Had the girl been nice to her lately only to recruit her as a servant for her family's rich friends?

"Emilie?"

"I'm deciding." As they reached the open deck, Emilie turned and studied Rosamund closely. Rosamund allowed it, looking back absolutely straight-faced.

There could be another explanation, Emilie thought. Maybe Rosamund's niceness was an apology for the incident in the toilet room. Maybe she'd tried to get Emilie a job as a way of making amends.

"All right," said Emilie. "I'm not mad at you, Rosamund."

The taller girl let out her breath. "Good. I'm glad." She turned to leave.

"And thank you," Emilie added.

Rosamund answered with a raised hand and kept walking.

Watching her go, Emilie was bothered by something. If the Albrechts were so grand, why weren't they traveling in pri-vate cabins like the Blumenfelds?

* * *

The wind rose again, filling the great white sails and driving the *Velma* westward. The sky was swept clear of clouds, and for days the endless ocean waves sparkled in the sun. Emilie spent as much time as possible on deck, trailed by Lotte Stein, Otto, and soon Elise and Stefan Blumenfeld. It was pure fun—until Meta Borner joined them.

"So you're Meta?" Otto asked the young woman. She'd just delighted a number of passengers with a dramatic telling of "The Bremen Town Musicians," one of the folktales collected by the Brothers Grimm. "Funny you have the same name as our mama."

"Yes, funny, isn't it?" The girl giggled impishly and met Emilie's eyes.

Nerves squirmed like spider legs in Emilie's middle. Meta sensed Papa hadn't heard the ticket story, and Meta was taking advantage of it. Suddenly, all at once, Emilie knew how to handle her.

Jumping up from her cross-legged position, she cried vivaciously, "Oh, yes. Meta is my neighbor in the cabin." She flounced over to the young man at the edge of Meta's audience, whom she'd got a good look at during the dancing. "And this is Meta's husband. Have you seen the two of them dance? Next time we have music, they must show us!" In triumph, she smiled at Meta. For now, at least, she'd ended any threat that Meta would call herself Borner.

Meta smiled back thinly, lips closed.

But Emilie wasn't done with Meta yet. She cornered her later in the cabin. "We can talk here, or on deck. You pick."

Meta looked Emilie up and down. "You know, I'm glad I'm not your mama. You're a handful."

"If I bear responsibility for giving you the ticket, then you do also for accepting it. The power struggle between us is over. Now, do you want to have it out in here, or on deck?"

Meta's mouth hardened, but she answered what Emilie expected. "On deck."

Emilie turned to leave the cabin.

"Quietly. Or I'll see to it your father learns the whole story."

Emilie whirled. "No more fear of being a stowaway?" Meta flinched. "I mean to tell Papa anyway. Now, do you want Frau Bauer and the others to wander in and hear too? Or are you coming?"

By the time the two got out on deck, Emilie had almost lost the taste for what she wanted to say. But she forged ahead.

"Meta, we're both afraid. You threaten to tell Papa what I've done unless I keep sharing food and clothes with you."

"You owe—" Meta began.

"And I don't want you to tell on me. Papa will say I didn't think. Maybe he could have gotten a refund on Mama's ticket! But I'm not sharing food, and Mama's clothes and good hair-brush, only to keep you quiet. I do it because it's right." She took a breath. "Christ taught us to share."

"You bet it's right," said Meta, but her tone had no fire. Her brown eyes stayed fixed on Emilie.

"You don't have to scare me into helping you," Emilie said. "I have a responsibility. And if you'd be a little grateful once in a while, I might even help you because I like you."

Meta gaped at her.

Emilie surprised even herself with her next words. "God is providing for you, Meta, and for your baby. He gave you Mama's ticket, to keep you with your husband. He's providing what you need on the ship. So don't thank me; I don't care. But won't you at least thank Him?"

Emilie took several steps backward, then turned and walked away. She had to think. If Mama's leaving had provided Meta's way to America, then St. Paul's words to the early church must really be true: All things must work together for good, for people like Mama who love God and are called according to His purpose.

Strolling in the breeze, Emilie felt easier now, about Karl's and Erich's refusal to emigrate, and Mama's search for them. Surely God was at work. And surely she would have no more problems with Meta.

But she forgot her resolve to tell Papa what she'd done with Mama's ticket.

*　　*　　*

"Emilie, you've become a regular Pied Piper of Hamelin," Della Jurgen teased one day in the dining hall. The cabin passengers sat at long tables, eating ox meat and rice for the midday meal.

"Oh, I hope not, Frau Jurgen!" Emilie protested in mock horror. "After all, the Pied Piper lured the children away from Hamelin forever."

"And you can count on us to keep showing up again," Otto joked. Wielding his vinegar bottle like a saltshaker, he doused his meal liberally. "If I can't have sauerkraut, I guess I'll have *sauer Ochs* and *sauer Reis.*"

"Otto," Papa admonished. Instantly the boy's face straightened and his hand stilled.

"Well, then I stand corrected," Frau Jurgen replied lightly. "But you can't deny, Emilie, the children follow you everywhere." The young woman looked at Heidi meaningfully. But Heidi, hunched over her tin plate, didn't see.

And she didn't speak. She only chewed a glob of rice, tired brown curls hanging in her eyes and tears running down her cheeks. Emilie suspected Heidi had been disciplined for her constant whining about the ship's food. Just as her heart went out to the little girl, Heidi stuck out her tongue and let a wad of starchy paste plop to her plate. Emilie's stomach jerked. Even Otto, not easily sickened, let out a groan.

Frau Jurgen excused herself and led Heidi from the table, bracing her hand against the small of her own back as she lumbered out of the dining hall. Emilie, distressed over how thin Heidi had become, could barely eat another bite herself.

She went straight to the cabin after the meal, hoping to find Heidi and her mother resting, or sharing a story, or eating something that wasn't greasy or suspected of being boiled in sea water. What she found was an almost empty room and Heidi alone, beside Emilie's bed, kneeling over Mama's trunk.

Concern flooded Emilie. Was Heidi looking for food? Could the Jurgens be running low, because Heidi ate so little of the ship's food? "Heidi? Do you need something, *Liebchen?*"

But as she stooped beside Heidi, she saw that the little girl didn't care about Mama's trunk. It was the shorter china trunk she'd managed to pull out from under the bed. She had unfastened one latch.

"Oh, Heidi, that's just dishes." She snapped the catch closed again and pushed the trunk back under the berth. "I wish it was a whole trunk full of good things to eat, but it's only things to eat *on*. Pretty silly, isn't it?"

Heidi burst into fresh, quiet weeping.

Emilie's heart began to hammer. "Heidi, I have zwieback yet, and some dried figs. You know, Jesus ate figs."

"Jesus isn't real!"

Emilie swallowed. "Where's your mama, Heidi?"

Heidi shook with sobs. "Toilet." Emilie was about to suggest other food when Heidi continued. "I don't want anything to eat."

"A story, then? Frau Bauer has both volumes of *Grimm's Fairy Tales.*"

"I don't like Frau Bauer. She's mean."

"Why no, Heidi. She's plain-speaking, but she's kind."

"Besides, then that girl from the cellar will come, and the rich ones will come, and I don't want them!"

Emilie sank back on her heels. Here was another problem. Heidi had expected them to be a twosome on the ship, and she was jealous of the other children. Frau Jurgen's attempt to interest Heidi in joining the "Pied Piper" had completely backfired.

Emilie reached out to stroke Heidi's curls, not as clean as they once were. "Heidi, I'm sorry this trip is not fun for you." She stood as Frau Jurgen entered the cabin, looking worn. "If you want to take a nap," she addressed Heidi's mother, "I'll take Heidi on deck awhile."

Heidi whipped her head back and forth.

"She can stay." Frau Jurgen sat on her bunk and lowered herself gingerly, her full belly hanging almost over the side. Emilie watched in fascination as the baby moved, a fan-shaped ripple under Frau Jurgen's ribs, like the waves of the sea. "I don't know that I can fall asleep anyway," the woman said. "I can only try."

As Emilie left the cabin, she breathed a prayer not only for Heidi, but also for her mother.

Chapter Eight

"These people are called Turners?" Emilie asked Papa as they, with Lotte, watched the gymnastic troupe perform on deck.

Papa nodded. They had been on the ocean for nearly four weeks. The lines between Papa's nose and the ends of his mustache had deepened, and there were scattered gray whiskers in his new, grizzled beard. "I wish Karl were here to see them. Then again, I don't."

Emilie spoke quietly, "I don't understand, Papa."

"They're much more than an athletic society." Papa paused as the eight men, dressed in identical white pants, shirts, red belts, and patterned ties began to form a pyramid. "They believe in a united Germany, and in government control of most business and industry. I wish Karl could see that many of these political liberals are emigrating."

Emilie gazed, captivated, at the finished pyramid. Four of the men stood on each other's shoulders, while the other four hung off the sides. Hands were interlocked, legs were braced on shoulders or feet planted on thighs. Their formation was perfectly matched on either side, their balance flawless.

"And why are you glad Karl can't see them?" Emilie asked. The pyramid broke up and the men began to juggle weighted balls and tapered pins.

Papa's answer came slowly. "Turners trust in physical fitness, human reasoning, and intellectual study to improve the human race. There's nothing wrong with these things, you understand. But they are tools only. The trust must be placed in God."

Emilie wrinkled her brow. "And you think if Karl were here, he'd want to be like these men who don't trust in God?"

"Some are actually hostile to Christians," Papa replied. "Especially to pastors."

When the Turner exhibition ended, Lotte took Emilie aside. "Your papa is right. The Turners travel in steerage, and so does the pastor. Some heckle him and other believers constantly."

Emilie had been curious about steerage, and now her fascination mushroomed. "Will you take me down there? I want to see."

"Why?" Lotte asked. "You're in a cabin. You don't have to go down there ever."

"But I want to see," Emilie implored her. "I want to see what the whole ship is like."

Lotte studied Emilie. "All right. Maybe it's a good idea." She stepped through a hatch, and Emilie followed her down a flight of stairs to the steerage level. Before her feet even reached the floor, Emilie realized she was entering another world. The first thing that hit her was the smell.

It was a combination of all the smells on the ship—seasick smells, privy smells, cooking smells—and much stronger than anything Emilie had known in the cabin.

"With just a couple of openings in the ceiling, the place airs out poorly," Lotte said.

Emilie barely heard. She was taking in the endless rows of double-decker bunks. Neither the sleepers on the bottom nor the top had headroom to sit. Rosamund Albrecht's venomous threat about cracking her head in steerage came flooding back.

Those who were sitting leaned into the aisle to converse or bicker with their neighbors.

"You clergy are the blind leading the blind," a man in Turner pants taunted the Lutheran pastor. "You preach blind faith in a God who will take away all your troubles. How can you sleep at night?"

"You do not know your Bible," countered the pastor. "Only religious leaders without true faith are blind."

"It is not my Bible," jeered the first man. The buzz of argument continued.

What little floor room the passengers had was stuffed with trunks and duffels. A few flimsy screens isolated the toilets. But what made Emilie gasp in horror were the people lying in the beds. Though few tried to sleep at this time of day, several bunks held three, even four, curled up, stretched out, limbs entangled. Men, women, young, old—mixed together.

"We have—we have two men's cabins and a women's cabin," Emilie faltered.

"Yes," Lotte said simply. "Here, there's no privacy. Married, single, it doesn't matter. But even I am luckier than some. I share a bunk with a little girl and two women now. Mama and I used to have a man with us."

Emilie shuddered. "It's not—it just isn't—proper."

Lotte didn't take offense. "Being proper down here would be hard. That's why Mama and I aren't Christians. Proper costs money. We have to make do."

Emilie's mouth opened, but at first nothing came out. "I've wanted to meet your mama. She must feel better by now, doesn't she? Why didn't she come up to see the Turners?"

Lotte's smile flickered. "My papa was a Turner. He ran off before I was born. She doesn't care much for Turners."

Uneasiness stirred in Emilie. Who did Lotte's mother like? And would Karl turn into one of these people Lotte's mother—and his own papa—wouldn't care for?

"You're thinking we're not so equal anymore," Lotte said softly.

"No!" Emilie protested. "That's not what I'm thinking."

"Mama's still poorly. That's why she's in the bunk with just one man now. He's poorly too."

"Not still seasick?"

"I need to see how she's doing." Lotte wound her way up the aisle. Emilie followed, accidentally kicking a box and tripping on a burlap sack. "No, Emilie, I think she is more than seasick." Lotte stooped beside two sweaty, gray-skinned people in a lower bunk. "When I was seasick, I didn't get so feverish."

The woman lay closest to the aisle, and stirred at Lotte's voice. "Lotte, child?"

"Mama, please come walking," Lotte pleaded. "On deck. You need fresh air."

The woman shook her head. Emilie heard the scritch-scratching of hair on the rough pillow. "I can't. The cabin folk—panic."

"We can't worry about them, Mama!"

Lotte's mother shook her head.

"Then you must eat," Lotte urged. "People who eat are the ones who stay well." Lotte straightened and looked at Emilie. "Noontime is coming. I must go up and cook for Mama."

Emilie was amazed at the strength of this girl who seemed no older than Otto. "I have an idea. I can get your mama some lunch from the dining hall. In the forenoon we just get coffee and white bread, and at supper, soup or tea. But now there'll be beans or peas, maybe pork. Then you won't have to cook."

"But won't they serve you only a portion for yourself?"

Emilie shrugged. "I can miss a meal. We have bread and dried foods with us, anyway. Don't you?"

To her relief, Lotte nodded.

"It's settled, then. I'll meet you on deck, at the hatch, as soon after noon as I can."

Lotte eyed her soberly. "Do you pity us, Emilie Borner?"

Emilie, to her surprise, felt the prick of anger. "Are you too proud to take food from me? Do you think I look down on you? Well, if cabin people are proud, and you also are proud—what does that say? Equal. We are equal."

The smaller girl didn't answer.

"Before I go," Emilie said, "show me which bunk is yours."

Lotte looked mystified. "Why?"

"Just show me. Please?"

Lotte walked her to the foot of the stairs, and on the way pointed out an empty upper bunk. While the bedding was far from pure white, it didn't look particularly soiled.

"Noon," Emilie reminded, as she climbed the stairs to the

deck. Lotte stayed below, watching.

An idea was stirring in Emilie. She knew how to show Lotte, maybe even a few Turners, that Christianity was about bearing others' burdens, not about being proper or escaping burdens altogether.

She knew exactly what she was going to do.

* * *

After delivering a bowl of pork and barley to Lotte, Emilie borrowed Papa's Bible and made her way to the Blumenfelds' cabins. She read to Elise and Stefan every day before their afternoon naps, and she looked forward to it.

"This is a story about King David," Emilie began, as the three snuggled against the plump pillows on Elise's bed. Bracing her hand on the bed to position herself, Emilie heard a faint jingling and felt the press of coins under her palm.

"Someone dropped money on the bed."

"Mama did," said Stefan. "She drops money a lot. She can probably stop now."

Emilie had no idea what he meant, but she had noticed money lying around the Blumenfelds' cabins before. Sometimes as much as a whole *Taler* was secreted near a picture frame, or under a hairbrush, or on the floor beside a wardrobe door. Maybe the Blumenfelds simply had so much money that it collected in their corners like dust.

Emilie moved the money near the end of the bed, where the parents would see it. "This is a story about King David," she repeated. "Only this was before he became king, when he was a shepherd boy."

Emilie launched into the story of David and Goliath, and Stefan laughed heartily at the stone from David's slingshot piercing Goliath's forehead and killing him.

"Ros'und never tells a God story," Elise said softly.

Emilie met the little girl's wide eyes. "Rosamund? Does she tell you any stories?"

Elise nodded.

"A time or two," said her more talkative brother.

Surely Frau Blumenfeld wouldn't pay two girls to play with Elise and Stefan. But the children would know nothing about that. "I'm glad you see it's a God story, not just a sling-shot story," Emilie told them. "Remember how David said he was standing up for Israel? He said, 'I come in the name of the Lord Almighty!'"

At her shout, the door swung open, and there stood Frau Blumenfeld. The woman's eyebrows jumped high, pushing her forehead into rolls. "Emilie, what are you reading?" Frau Blumenfeld crossed the room in three strides and snatched the Bible.

"Please, it was David and Goliath," stammered Emilie.

"Not one of the more ridiculous stories, but incredible all the same." Frau Blumenfeld's tone was spirited. Then she softened. "Emilie. I'm partly to blame. I should have told you we're Free Thinkers. We don't hold with any tales about a god, and we certainly don't teach them to our children."

"I—I'm sorry," said Emilie, though she wasn't sure it was true.

"Apology accepted," Frau Blumenfeld said warmly. "Just be sure it doesn't happen again." The woman then saw the money lying near the foot of the bed. Picking it up, she pocketed it, and looked thoughtfully at Emilie.

*　　*　　*

Clouds were rolling in, like piles of dirty linen, as Emilie and Lotte Stein walked on deck.

"I would like to trade places with you," Emilie said, "for one night."

Lotte looked at Emilie as if she'd gone crazy. "Why would you ever do that?"

"Well," Emilie said, "you sleep in steerage every night. Why can't I for one night? And you can have a bed to yourself."

If Emilie had thought Lotte would jump at the chance, she didn't. "For one night, you want to know what it's like to be me."

"Does that insult you?" Emilie grasped her arm. "Suppose I

didn't care how dirty a hole you slept in? Suppose I thought steerage was beneath me? Wouldn't that insult you more?"

Lotte wavered. "Mama might need me."

"She would tell you to go sleep in my bed. I can check on your mama."

They fell silent, gazes locked.

"You mean it?" breathed Lotte.

"Absolutely." The embarrassment she'd begun to feel was swept away in relief.

Lotte could no longer hold back a smile. "Thank you, Emilie. A bed to myself, above deck, will be heaven."

* * *

Emilie didn't reconsider her offer until, in her nightdress, she shakily descended the steps into steerage. She knew no one down here. Would people stare, demand to know her name, make her repeat her peculiar offer to Lotte over and over? Maybe the Lutheran pastor would help her.

Emilie first made her way down the aisle toward Lotte's mother. Though people hung out of their bunks talking, no one exclaimed or even seemed to notice her. She was just another body passing by. Many were dressed much as she was and, by the looks of the valises and parcels she had to dodge, had just as many belongings. Emilie realized most of the steerage passengers were no poorer than she. They had simply chosen a cheaper way to make the crossing.

Lotte's mother still lay next to the sick man, eyes closed. Her skin clung tightly to her jaw and cheekbones. Her throat worked as if she might cough, but she made no sound.

"Careful there, *Fraulein*," came a man's voice behind her. "You can't help them by catching what they've got."

Emilie straightened. The ill woman had just received water from Lotte anyway. She wanted nothing now.

It was late, and two of the oil lamps were extinguished. People began to lie down. New sounds began—quiet sobbing, hawking and spitting, scratching, praying, appeals to shut up.

Emilie could no longer avoid climbing into Lotte's bunk. If she waited for complete darkness she'd never find her way.

Stomach churning, Emilie waded toward the bunk Lotte had pointed out. Two girls of marriageable age were already in it, and now she'd have to explain herself.

"Please," said Emilie. Both girls looked at her, not unkindly. "I've traded places—" But that was as far as she got. A hand clamped onto her arm and whirled her around.

"Lotte!" Emilie was thunderstruck at the girl's tear-streaked face.

"Go upstairs!" she cried. "Go on, go. Get out!"

"Lotte! What happened?"

"I should have known. Go. Just go."

"Lotte—"

"*Lebewohl!*" Lotte punctuated her good-bye with a shove toward the stairs. Emilie stumbled, losing a wooden slipper. It shot under someone's berth.

"*Hei!* A fight!" someone cheered.

"No! No brawling!"

Frantic, Emilie scrambled for her slipper.

"*Hei!* Those are my things!"

"Get out!" screamed Lotte.

"*Hei!* Wild girl! Into the bunk."

Another light went out.

Emilie lunged for the stairs and galloped up, leaving her slipper behind. Almost diving onto the deck, she let her breath out hard. Here would be peace. But it wasn't so. There was a crowd to meet her, including the Albrechts, Frau Bauer, several sailors, Otto—and Papa.

"What is going on, daughter?" he demanded, holding a lamp high. At that moment Emilie saw who was standing beside him. "This woman claims you've infested the cabin with plague. She also claims her name is Meta Borner."

Chapter Nine

"If your girl has picked up lice, or worse, she's not coming back in the cabin!" called Frau Albrecht.

"Oh, it is worse!" Meta shrilled. "That other girl's mama is sick to death down there, and she brought the scourge up to us!"

Frau Bauer, wrapped in a fringed shawl, strode forward and stuck her round face into Meta's. "Your husband sleeps in steerage. You dance with him every time some lout blows a mouth organ. Then you come into the cabin and put on a dress that little girl gives you." Frau Bauer jabbed a finger sideways at Emilie. "Maybe it's time we accuse you of spreading disease."

Meta shrank back in alarm. Frau Bauer scanned the entire assembly. "Use your heads. We're in no more danger than we've ever been. Let's get on back to bed."

"Maybe we ought to get rid of them both," came an answering shout. "If they prefer steerage—"

"*Ja,* the one with child is pretending to be someone else!"

"Something is unseemly with her. It might be worth the captain's while to check her ticket."

Meta was shaking, but fire kindled in her eyes. "My ticket is valid!"

Emilie's glance moved to Papa, and his to her.

"Enough." Papa raised his hands for quiet. "Her ticket is not an issue."

"Says you."

"How would you know?"

"I know," said Papa. He addressed the newly arrived captain. "You, Captain, might care to check it, though of course it was

70

found to be in order when she boarded." He paused. "Emilie."

Emilie stepped closer to him. She felt wobbly. "Yes, Papa."

"Have you been sleeping in a steerage berth with a sick woman?"

"No, Papa. I was going to sleep in Lotte's bunk. She shares with three girls. But I never even got in."

There was some murmuring from the crowd.

Papa lifted his head. "Frau Bauer? Did the girl Lotte lie down in my daughter's bunk?"

"*Ja.* But you never saw such a ruckus. She was driven straight out, poor waif." Frau Bauer snorted.

Papa turned back to Meta. "Young woman? Along with using my wife's things, have you brought to your cabin anything from steerage that your husband had in his luggage? On his person? In his bunk, which he shares with complete strangers? Anything at all?"

Meta swallowed. Then she nodded.

The murmurs and gasps grew. "What is it?" some cried. "What foul thing did you bring to the cabin?"

"What does it matter?" Papa asked sharply. "Is everyone in the cabin clean and healthy?"

The deck quieted. Only wind and waves could be heard.

Papa turned back to Meta. "You do see how foolish it would be to complain any further? About anything?"

Miserably, Meta nodded again.

"Likewise the rest of you?" Papa addressed the people on deck. They began to shuffle toward the cabins. It struck Emilie that Rosamund Albrecht had watched everything, and hadn't made the slightest friendly gesture.

"My daughter will change her bedding before she lies down," Papa called after them. "And that should end the matter."

"Good work, Herr Borner," the captain congratulated Papa. "Anytime we can quell a riot, it's appreciated." He paused. "As for the woman's ticket: If it were fake, she'd never have made it onto my ship. She can call herself King Friedrich Wilhelm IV, for all I care. If she's got a ticket, she's a passenger."Taking his leave, the captain disappeared into the night.

The wind blew steadily now, and Emilie hugged herself. Toes on her bare foot curling, she took one step toward the cabin.

"Emilie."

Only she and Papa were left on deck. Emilie turned.

"Did you think I would scold because you'd given away Mama's ticket?" Papa lowered the lamp from his face.

She nodded.

"You're right," Papa said. "I would have said you were tempting someone completely unprepared for travel. I would have said you were encouraging an illegal emigration. I would have said you didn't understand the consequences. Just as you didn't understand the consequences of trading bunks with a steerage passenger." Papa paused. "But I suspect you've learned about consequences on your own."

Emilie nodded.

"The girl who calls herself Meta, and who uses your mama's things, may be flighty, fearful, pesky, even a bit simple-minded. But at least she doesn't seem to be a criminal."

Emilie winced. "No, Papa."

"Why did you do it, child?"

"She was weeping on the dock," Emilie pleaded. "I had the means to keep a family together, if only I gave her the ticket we didn't need."

Papa said nothing for the longest time.

"Papa?"

"Out of one family's separation, another was united."

Emilie couldn't answer.

Suddenly Papa's hand dropped to her shoulder. "God bless you, girl. And continue to use you to His glory."

Filled with wonder, Emilie made her way back to the cabin. She didn't see the lightning that forked the sky.

* * *

At dawn, the storm broke. Emilie woke to feel the *Velma* bucking like a thousand-ton stallion. The cabin door crashed open and Frau Bauer barreled in. "Get up and empty the chamber pots, or you'll wish you had."

Women began stirring. The whole room swayed.

"Just don't go out on the open deck!" Frau Bauer hollered. "You'll be swept away."

Emilie's trip out of the cabin was brief and terrifying. Shoeless, teetering, she managed to glimpse a small section of the deck. Higher than the rail loomed a wall of gray water, as if the ship were sailing in a trough. Rain slashed the gleaming planks, spraying her with a fine mist. She scurried back inside.

"This is where your rope comes in handy," yelled Frau Bauer. "Everybody sit on one of your trunks. The others you'll have to tie down."

Emilie immediately saw why. As the ship listed to one side, the cabin slanted. Though the berths were bolted to the floor, boxes and trunks peeked out from under those on Emilie's wall, then skidded toward the berths on Frau Bauer's.

The china! Bracing Mama's trunk with her body, Emilie flipped it open and hauled out, hand over hand, seemingly endless lengths of rope. She had to tie down the china. If Karl's inheritance should break—well, it would give a sick feeling in the pit of the stomach, a feeling that the Borners themselves were broken apart with no fixing. She couldn't let it happen.

Outside, the wind whistled through the planks, the sails, the rigging, sliding up and down an eerie musical scale. Cracking sounds began overhead. Voices exclaimed. Heidi Jurgen cried.

"Meta," Emilie gasped. "Help me tie down the china."

"What do you care about china?" Meta moaned, clutching her bed frame.

"Maybe I don't want the trunk to roll down the aisle and smash somebody's head," Emilie shouted, as it banged smartly into someone's shins. "You're supposed to be an adult. Help me!"

Meta fumbled for an end of rope. "String this through the handles of the trunk. Tie it to the leg of the bed."

Emilie set off after the trunk. But as the ship rose and sank, people began falling. Frau Bauer and Della Jurgen extinguished the oil lamps, plunging the cabin into darkness. It took all Emilie's strength to push the china trunk back to Meta's bed and implore her to sit on it. Then there was nothing anyone could do but hang on for the ride.

* * *

"...And protect Papa, and Otto, and the people in steerage," Emilie prayed as the storm raged. Wailing filled the cabin, some of it coming from Frau Albrecht and Rosamund. Catholic passengers prayed the rosary over and over. Emilie had heard Frau Jurgen praying too, but it seemed that every time she started, Heidi would break out in fresh sobs. Soon Frau Jurgen fell silent.

Little by little, Emilie had looped rope around Mama's trunk and the leg of the bed, and now she dared crawl through the dark to Frau Bauer, herself perched on a trunk wedged between two beds. "What do you think is going on in steerage, Frau Bauer?"

Frau Bauer snorted. "Funny it's you asking. Isn't it your friend Meta who's got a husband down there?"

"I was afraid to upset her," confided Emilie. Frau Bauer's snort was more of a laugh this time. "Young girl, you are a breath of fresh air even in a reeking box like this. In steerage," she mused, "I expect the privies have sloshed over by now."

"Ooohh," groaned Emilie.

"I expect the cooking pots and spoons and even small trunks are floating."

"Floating?"

"The water pouring onto the deck goes right down the hole. Oh, they close the hatch by the stairs, but they can't shut every opening or the people will suffocate."

Emilie felt numb.

"If you've got any praying left in you, girl, pray for them."

Wriggling back to her bunk, Emilie did. "Jesus, once You stopped a storm when the apostles were afraid . . ."

"Jesus isn't real," grieved Heidi Jurgen, followed by crooning sounds from her mother.

". . . so I know the wind and waves are under Your control," Emilie went on.

"Della, wouldn't it serve your daughter better if you face up to what she's saying," exploded Frau Albrecht, "instead of teaching her a lie?"

A din of protest rose. Catholics, Lutherans, Reformed, and those who simply respected a mother's attempt to comfort a child, shouted her down.

"O Lord," Emilie prayed, "we're just a tiny boat in the Atlantic. Calm the storm. And please show Heidi that You are real. And Lotte. And the Blumenfelds. And the Turners. And the Albrechts."

And the storm eased. Emilie realized it was so when she caught herself drifting between sleep and prayer, prone on the hard floor. She lifted her head in time to hear Frau Jurgen pray softly, "And please, *mein Gott,* stop the pain."

Chapter Ten

By Sunday morning, September 30, the sun had come out again, the deck had dried, and the sails of the *Velma* swelled with a cooler autumn wind. At church service, a woman gave Emilie a pair of shoes. The worship had barely ended, and people were moving aside the crates they'd been sitting on, when Frau Albrecht came on deck and accosted Della Jurgen.

"To see your child decline pains me so," Emilie heard the older woman say. "For her own good, can't you at least admit that God might be wishful thinking?"

Frau Jurgen colored. "I can't admit to what I don't believe," she said calmly.

"But just what is it you *do* believe? Some of you Reformed, and some of the Catholics, sit in the service, while others will hardly breathe the same air as a Lutheran pastor. Who is right? Della, I'm just concerned about you, that's all."

"Just concerned," Reinhard Jurgen repeated, suddenly appearing behind his wife. "Then your question about what we believe isn't sincere?"

Frau Albrecht blushed. "I just think you should stop and consider what you believe, that's all."

"And I just had to find out if you were possibly seeking God. Since you are merely a persecutor, excuse us. My wife is tired." The couple moved toward the cabins.

"God didn't stop the storm!" Frau Albrecht looked around at everyone now, catching Emilie, too, in her glance.

Emilie was mortified to hear a snort of disdain from Otto. "Well, the storm is over. This is news to you?"

"Otto!" Emilie cried.

"What if the storm was still going on?" Otto bellowed, as Papa lifted him and removed him from the crowd. "What would you say then?"

Emilie's hands rose to her mouth.

Pastor Dallmann, the Lutheran pastor, approached Frau Albrecht, whose eyes shot sparks after Otto. "Maybe it's all well and good for me to say this, since I'm not the boy's papa, but the boy is right. If we choose to believe God doesn't care, we won't see Him, no matter what good or bad happens around us."

Frau Albrecht's eyes skittered away from the pastor. "The storm raged for twenty-four hours," she muttered. "So many fools in the cabin sniveled endlessly, calling for God's help. God didn't stop the storm."

"I think you mean God didn't prevent the storm," Pastor Dallmann said. "If He prevented all storms, when could He show you His comfort?"

Emilie heard no more. The pastor and Frau Albrecht took several steps down the deck, out of her sight. She knew she shouldn't eavesdrop, and it was time to join Papa and Otto for lunch. Solemnly, Emilie thought of her brother. She would tell him what the pastor had said.

* * *

When Emilie visited the Blumenfeld children, she always entered by the parents' cabin. Today Frau Blumenfeld seemed pre-occupied, bustling back and forth through the door to the children's room before letting Emilie pass. *Maybe she is busy straightening up after the storm,* Emilie thought. Her cabin still looked a bit like a tossed salad, but here things appeared quite orderly.

"I brought the Brothers Grimm today," Emilie greeted the children as they snuggled on Elise's bed.

"Rosamund brought that once," said Stefan. "You can't read the same story she did."

"But Ros'und didn't bring it today," added Elise.

Emilie turned to the little girl. "Rosamund was here today?"

"She just left," Stefan said. "But she didn't read to us. She just talked on and on to Mama, talk, talk, talk. Rosamund is a *Dummkopf.*" Stefan gave a silly smile, clearly asking Emilie to agree that Rosamund was a blockhead.

"Emilie." Elise pulled gently at her elbow. "I like God stories better."

Emilie felt a chill. "Well—today we have the Grimms."

"I know why. Mama will throw you out if you tell God stories," Stefan declared.

"I was scared when we had the storm," Elise whispered.

"So was I, *Liebchen.*"

"Mama says God was no help at all."

No wonder the Blumenfelds and Albrechts got along. "No help?"

"Mama and Papa say a good God wouldn't let bad things happen," said Stefan.

Emilie thought hard about what Pastor Dallmann had said: If He prevented all storms, when could He show you His comfort?

"If we never had trouble, we'd forget all about God," Emilie said. "People wouldn't be as close, either, because they'd never have to help each other with hard things." She glanced gratefully at her new shoes. "All through the storm I prayed, and I felt closer to the other passengers and to God. That helped me be less afraid—"

The door burst open. "All of which proves nothing," seethed Frau Blumenfeld. "A made-up god will work for that."

Emilie broke out in a sweat. Her heart raced. She knew she would be fired.

"And He is made up, isn't He, Emilie Borner?"

Emilie swallowed, struggling to open her dry mouth.

"How could you do what you've done and then tell my children there's a God?"

Emilie's insides spun in confusion. "What I've done? Are you mad at me for something more?"

"You're a thief!" yelled Frau Blumenfeld. Emilie shrank back in dread. Elise began to cry, and Stefan wasn't far behind.

"A thief!" Emilie made herself rise up out of the pillow. "But I didn't steal anything."

"You've seen money lying around, here and there, ever since you started working for us," Frau Blumenfeld spat. "Do you think we are so casual, so careless? It was a test of your honesty! You resisted a long time, but finally even the Christian gave in to temptation. The money is gone."

"Please," Emilie said desperately. "The storm. Your money must have fallen everywhere in the cabin—"

"You are through here," interrupted Frau Blumenfeld. "You will leave—now. And stay away from my children for the duration of this trip."

Grabbing Frau Bauer's storybook, Emilie scrambled off Elise's bed, leaving the two sobbing children behind. Once she got between Frau Blumenfeld and the door she called back, "I didn't steal money, Elise, Stefan. I didn't." Dodging Frau Blumenfeld's clutches, she whirled and fled the cabin.

*　*　*

She told Papa without delay. He believed her.

Not much else happened that was good. Lotte Stein avoided her, seeming to prefer Frau Bauer's company. Heidi Jurgen perked up a bit when she saw that Lotte, Elise, and Stefan weren't around, but by now she looked so spindly that Emilie was afraid of malnutrition.

Rosamund Albrecht started hanging near, asking ardently why Emilie was upset.

Frau Bauer told her that Lotte's mother had died.

"No!" exclaimed Emilie.

"*Ach*, it was fated, girl," admonished Frau Bauer. "The man next to her went, too."

Emilie's shoulders slumped. Then something occurred to her. "People can't get buried on a ship."

"Well, now, if you've got a pastor he can say the same nice words on sea or land. But there's nothing for the bodies except to be taken out in bags and dropped over the side."

Emilie shuddered, but her eyes went to the waves. "Did Lotte watch?"

"Child, it's all *you* can do not to run to the side. I think you know the answer."

"Then Lotte, such a little girl, has nobody."

Frau Bauer looked surprised. "Just how little do you think Lotte is?"

Emilie blinked. "Otto's age. Nine or ten."

"Lotte is fourteen, child."

"Older than I am?" She gasped.

"Does Lotte really have nobody?"

Emilie stared. "Well—she could come with us. I would beg Papa. But ever since we tried to trade beds, she can't bear the sight of me."

"You believe God cares, don't you? Let's give Him a chance to show what He can do."

Still staring, Emilie nodded thoughtfully.

* * *

Rosamund cornered her near the bow, away from most of the passengers. "You look so depressed lately," she cooed.

Emilie had had enough of the hovering. "Besides people I care about not doing very well, I'm sure the Blumenfelds have told you they fired me. They think I stole money, but I didn't. Of course I'm depressed."

"I can sympathize," said Rosamund. "It's your word against theirs. Too bad most passengers believe the Blumenfelds. After all, people figure you could use a few *Talers* more than your wage, and . . ." Rosamund lifted her eyebrows.

Emilie's heart thudded. "How many people believe I'm a thief? Frau Bauer believes me!" she cried.

"How much help is that?" Rosamund shrugged. "Frau Bauer is as common as dirt."

"Rosamund!" Emilie turned on her angrily, but Rosamund didn't flinch. "If Frau Bauer is so common, why do you sleep only five berths away from her? If you Albrechts are so grand, why don't you travel next door to the Blumenfelds? That's something I've been wondering about, and I'd really like to know."

Rosamund's nostrils flared. "Of all the—and to think I tried to be nice to you."

"Nice? First you either ignore me or insult me, then you act like one of my best friends, find me a job, go back to ignoring me, and now you've come around again. I have no idea what you'll do next. That's being nice?"

Rosamund pursed her mouth as if she'd sucked a pickle. "And to think I was afraid I'd come to like you. I needn't have bothered having such a conscience." Rosamund's eyes widened in the tiniest moment of panic. She regretted something she'd said.

Emilie pounced on it. "Conscience about what?" But Rosamund revealed nothing. "Why were you afraid you might like me? Am I so far beneath you that liking me would be such a shame?"

Suddenly her talk with Frau Jurgen about Rosamund, their first day in the cabin, came flooding back. She herself had suggested Rosamund thought her a commoner. Frau Jurgen had remarked that Rosamund was jealous of her happiness and her friends. Heidi's mother had said something else, too, something that now made Emilie quake.

"Did you persuade Frau Blumenfeld she needed a hired girl for the children?" Emilie's voice shook.

"Well, women of the better classes are accustomed to—"

"Hiring commoners."

"Well, yes," Rosamund chuckled. It was supposed to be derisive, but Emilie heard the tension.

Revenge. That was the word Frau Jurgen had used. Rosamund would deal with her jealousy of a commoner by cutting that commoner down to size.

"And do women of the better classes usually leave money lying around, to test their help?" Emilie asked.

"All the time."

Rosamund's answer was swift and self-satisfied. She could not resist sounding off as an expert on the better classes.

Emilie fastened her eyes on the waves. "And do girls from those same better classes usually visit the employer's children when the worker isn't there?"

No answer.

"For example, on the very morning the employer happens to find money missing?" Emilie spun toward Rosamund so hard her braids whipped the air. "You took the money! To disgrace me, because you hate me."

No denial came. The bottom dropped out of Emilie's stomach. Not only had she guessed right, but Rosamund hardly cared. Her eyes widened only briefly. Her mouth was set in triumph.

"And you had to let me know," Emilie said, "that you got me good."

"And so I did," Rosamund hissed. "And now you know your place, a girl as smart as you. Now you know."

*   *   *

Emilie did her crying in the cabin with Della Jurgen. "Of course I believe you didn't steal money," the young woman hushed her.

"Rosamund said the most awful thing." Emilie sniffled. "She said she was afraid she might get to like me."

Frau Jurgen laughed and hugged her hard. "Like you! What a scandal that would pose for the illustrious Rosamund." She grew thoughtful. "Emilie—suppose Rosamund came up with a scheme to get you hired by the Blumenfelds, and then fired in disgrace. She can't do that unless she introduces you. She can't do *that* unless she becomes friendly with you. Isn't that so?"

Emilie nodded.

"When did she first become friendly?"

Emilie thought back. "The first time we danced."

"You had fun that day, didn't you? With Rosamund and Otto? Rosamund had fun too. More than she planned on, I suspect. And if she grew to like you, how could she play an awful trick? She had to stay away from you after that day. She had to harden her heart; either that or give up her anger, admit you two could be friends, and she'd no longer be above you."

"We'd be equal," said Emilie.

"Just so."

Emilie took her time absorbing this. "The Blumenfelds would never believe Rosamund stole the money."

"You have no proof," her friend said faintly.

"I'd sound petty claiming Rosamund did it to get me in trouble." Emilie sighed. "The Blumenfelds think a Christian stole from them. Now they're farther than ever from believing in God."

Frau Jurgen shifted her bulk as she slumped on her bed. "Probably so."

"And so is any unbeliever who thinks I'm a thief."

"Emilie, those who refuse to believe in God find a million excuses for their refusal. Those who do believe, or want to, will not be hindered by what happened to you."

Emilie drew a shaky breath. She would accept this assurance. She met Frau Jurgen's eyes, and to her surprise found them creased with—pain?

"Are you all right?"

Frau Jurgen, pale again, smiled wanly. "God did more than stop the storm, that night last week. He also stopped the pains. But they came again. And went. And came. This time they're not going to leave." The woman shook her head.

"You mean—?"

"It shouldn't be my time for three weeks yet. We should have reached Wisconsin before the birth. But it's not going to be. Before we even sight land, this child will be born." Frau Jurgen lay back, grimacing, trying to smooth her breathing.

Emilie's heart turned over.

"Pray, Emilie."

"I will."

"Not for me," Frau Jurgen panted. "Pray for—my little—Heidi."

Chapter Eleven

Frau Bauer turned out to be a midwife.

"Sure, you can thank God for that," Frau Bauer told Emilie, as Della Jurgen leaned against her panting with the pain. "But thank Him for this: It's afternoon. We have sun. The good-for-nothings will clear out on deck. We won't have to fool with gawkers and screamers and fainters."

Frau Jurgen straightened and blinked; the pain, for now, was over. The two women resumed strolling the aisle between the bunks.

Frau Jurgen's labor had been going on for hours. So far she'd sat, walked, chatted, massaged her belly. She hadn't cried out once. It was Meta who'd fled, whimpering, from the cabin.

"You could learn something here, girl, in your condition," Frau Bauer had remarked tartly as Meta dashed for the door.

"Go on with you," Meta gasped. "You think if I spend one more second here I'll have the gumption to go through it when my time comes?" The cabin door slammed.

"City folk," Frau Bauer snorted.

Others had also made themselves scarce. Heidi's father had come to fetch her as soon as he heard the news. A few came in and out as they needed to, but relieved that the laboring woman had help, they left her alone. That help, Emilie thought with growing excitement, included herself. Frau Bauer had asked her to serve as assistant.

Now, the walking stopped. Della Jurgen collapsed against Frau Bauer's strong frame.

"*Ach*, those pains are good and strong and close together," said Frau Bauer. "It's high time I examined you." She began walking Frau Jurgen back to the bed.

The Albrechts, still puttering in their back corner, straightened abruptly. "Rosamund, we'll be leaving. This is no place for a young lady." Rosamund followed her mother up the aisle.

Young lady, thought Emilie. *Rosamund is being trained to forget the facts of life even she learned in the country.*

Frau Bauer ignored them. "Emilie, spread clean towels on the bed."

After helping Frau Jurgen into the bunk and laying a thin sheet across her, Frau Bauer stooped over the end of the bed and busied herself under the linen. "*Ach*, you're ready, Della." Frau Bauer's plain face glowed with triumph. "It's time to start bearing down each time the pain comes."

Frau Jurgen, her nightdress clammy, leaned back. She hardly had time to draw breath before a new pain was upon her. She pushed, clenching her teeth.

"Della, open your teeth. You want to grind them to powder?" Frau Bauer said.

Frau Jurgen pushed through several more pains.

The midwife frowned. "Baby's headfirst, but not moving down. Was it slow like this with your girl?"

Frau Jurgen shook her head. Another pain came. This time she gave a little shout as she curled her head forward.

"Emilie, support her neck and shoulders," urged Frau Bauer. "*Ja*, like so," she added, as Emilie nearly sat at the head of the bed. Della's skin felt hot through the thin nightgown. Her soft hair, now unruly, tickled Emilie's chin.

Frau Jurgen kept trying, but the baby wasn't coming.

Lord, please help it be born, Emilie prayed silently. She knew, though, that so many babies didn't come right. Her excitement was wiped out by a stab of fear.

But Frau Bauer hadn't yet run out of answers. "We will turn her on her side. Della, help us roll you over."

As Frau Jurgen wriggled, Emilie and Frau Bauer tipped her shoulders and hips until the weight of her stomach carried her over. Emilie felt sweat dribble down her sides. She swiped a finger across her upper lip.

"So." Frau Bauer gave a sharp, satisfied nod. "When it's taking awhile, it helps to change position."

The pains rolled on.

"Don't push with your face, Della. Push from the waist down." Frau Bauer fumbled under the covering again. She frowned.

O God, please don't do this, Emilie prayed. *Don't send Frau Jurgen's baby to the bottom of the ocean in a bag. Heidi will never get over it.*

She couldn't bear to form words about Frau Jurgen being put in a similar bag. She cut off her prayer abruptly.

After all, Mama had survived bad births. For the first time in months, Emilie thought of the three little grave markers, without names, that stood in a row in the cemetery back in Thuringen. One sister dead of disease, two brothers dead after harrowing births, all born during the seven-year span between Karl and Emilie. Yet Mama had been fine. Mama had gone on.

God, Emilie prayed, *if You love Heidi, don't do this.*

"Enough," Frau Bauer snapped, jerking Emilie from her thoughts. "Della, you must get up on your haunches. Do you hear me?"

Frau Jurgen had long ago given up speech, but she nodded.

"Emilie, we will support her one on each side." Frau Bauer bustled to the head of the bed, across from Emilie. "Put your left hand in the middle of her back. Let her grip your other arm. We will help her. *Eins, zwei, drei,* go."

Emilie staggered under Frau Jurgen's weight. Lift, she must lift.

"The pain again." Frau Jurgen sighed.

"We'll just hold you through this one," Frau Bauer said. "Emilie's got you. Don't you, Emilie?"

Emilie willed her knees not to buckle. "This is hard—" She stopped. She knew Frau Bauer wanted a cheerful answer. "Yes,

yes, I've got you," she puffed.

"You were going to say what?" Frau Bauer demanded.

"'This is harder than farm work,' maybe?"

To Emilie's complete astonishment, Frau Jurgen laughed. "If that's a sly way—of calling me a cow, I protest."

"Lift her, Emilie!"

Emilie lifted as never before.

"Here—now," Della groaned.

"All right, *push*," Frau Bauer ordered.

Frau Jurgen tucked her chin to her chest, held her breath, and bore down. Suddenly her chin shot up, her eyes bugged out. "It's coming!"

"Really?" gasped Emilie. "It's coming? Praise You, Lord!"

"Emilie!" Frau Bauer barked. "Get behind her and let her back easy." Frau Bauer fairly leaped to the foot of the bed.

"Head's out!" bawled Frau Bauer. "Della, it's got hair. Hanks of dark hair just like yours. One more push!"

Frau Bauer had hardly finished saying this when she lifted up a wet, bluish infant trailing a thick cord from its middle. The baby began to cry.

"It's a boy!" crowed Frau Bauer.

Emilie slowly released Frau Jurgen and her hands rose to her mouth. Her dismay at the child's color melted as a pink blush crept over his skin.

Frau Jurgen, trembling, reached out to take hold of the boy.

"God, You did not forget us," Emilie prayed. "You did not forget Heidi. This boy will not go to a nameless grave. Today, October 3, 1855, You did not forget."

The cabin door burst open.

"Land! Land!" a voice cried. "We have spied land!"

Chapter Twelve

Friday, October 5, 1855, the packet ship *Velma* entered New York Harbor. Every passenger, well or frail, steerage or cabin, first-timer or returnee, jammed the rails to see America at last. Almost no one broke the hush, not even two-day-old Josef Jurgen, sleeping tightly in the arms of his mother.

There was still so much water everywhere. But Emilie, at the bow rail, soon saw two slabs of land through a blue-gray mist, flat as mere blisters on the waves. To her left, low hills dipped up and down, while two islands loomed so close she thought they'd bump. Now the land squeezed toward the ship on both sides, now flared out again to reveal a familiar sight: ships of all sizes, all nations, coming and going. Piers poked the bobbing waves like the teeth of a giant comb, many more ships tucked into the slots. Straight ahead, buildings towered.

"Ahead there, that's where we must go," Lambert Albrecht said quietly. "They call it the Neu Jork State Immigration Station," he pronounced in labored English. "It wasn't open when I came before. It has only been operating two months."

Rosamund slunk near her father. "Oh, this is the place you told us about, Papa? Where they decide if you're good enough to be an American?"

"The red sandstone building," replied Herr Albrecht.

"And if you don't pass inspection, you get shipped back?" chirped Rosamund.

"Shush, daughter."

Seething, Emilie squinted at the many-sided building, which she guessed was an octagon. But she was nervous as well as angry. What if she wasn't good enough to be an

American? What if someone in her family wasn't?

The *Velma* dropped anchor in the bay. The passengers, Herr Albrecht said, would be ferried to the building. Crossing the ocean was not enough. Whether one could truly become an American would be decided here.

* * *

Beyond the wooden fence, inside the thick walls of the octagonal building, people and luggage were strewn everywhere. Offices, information booths, and medical exam rooms buzzed with activity.

Emilie glanced uneasily at her family's luggage, hoping it would be safe just sitting there. She spied Heidi Jurgen, to her amazement crouched again before the china trunk, fingering the latches.

"Heidi," said Emilie, kneeling beside her. "That's the trunk with the dishes, remember? Do you think they're pretty, is that it? I can show them to you when we get to Wisconsin."

Heidi shook her head violently.

Sighing, Emilie stood up. Maybe Heidi's presence would be a protection for the trunks. "Just don't open it," she said.

What she really wanted was to tell Heidi she missed her cheerful play, missed being called My Favorite Emilie. Would the inspectors here find Heidi odd, unfit to enter America? Emilie shuddered.

And how about the others? Among the *Velma's* passengers, good friendships and even love had blossomed. Farewells, sometimes tearful, had been said on the barge that had carried them to shore. Now would some not be admitted to the new land? Following Papa, Emilie scanned the crowd.

Lotte Stein, hand in hand with Frau Bauer, was just disappearing in another direction. No doubt she would never see them again. Frau Bauer had expressed good wishes, but the plucky young singer had said little more than *auf Wiedersehen.* The two had grown as close as mother and daughter, though, and that was no small thing.

"Emilie!"

Emilie's head jerked toward the voice. "Meta?"

The young woman, still wearing Mama's dress, broke away from her husband and hurried toward her. "Emilie—for all you have done—*danke schön.*"

Emilie's mouth fell open.

"I didn't know if I should keep your mama's clothes or return them, since I got them all dirty. They won't fit anyway before long, so I returned them." Meta gestured to Mama's trunk.

Emilie groped for words. "I—I'm glad I could help you, Meta. Have a good life in America."

After fervent thanks from the young husband, the couple was off. For many seconds, Emilie stared at the spot where they'd blended into the crowd.

* * *

Procedures at the New York State Immigration Station were surprisingly brief. Disease? No, the Borners, Albrechts, and Jurgens had none. Criminal record? No. Immoral behavior? Emilie just barely understood what this meant. Frau Albrecht screamed in outrage, and Otto darted forward hoping for a skirmish. No. Immoral behavior was not a problem. The travelers were free to go.

"Free?" breathed Emilie.

"And equal," Otto murmured to Rosamund. "You must be homesick already." Rosamund turned her back in disgust.

"What happens next?" Emilie asked Papa. She watched Herr Albrecht, grinning broadly, shake hands with a well-dressed man.

"We buy steamboat tickets to a place called Albany. From there we take a canal boat to," Papa paused to get the place names right, "Buffalo. Then another boat over the big lakes to Sheboygan, Wisconsin."

Emilie's knees wanted to buckle. Would there be no end to the miles of water? "How long will it all take, Papa?"

"Ten days, Herr Albrecht says. A day longer for him, since he will go to Chicago."

Herr Albrecht and the other man started off through the crowd. "Do we follow them? Are they leading us to the ticket place?" asked Emilie.

"No," Papa answered. "That man may be one of his business partners from Chicago, come to meet him. The Albrechts' plans may change. We go this way to purchase tickets." Papa pointed.

After the Borners and Jurgens bought tickets for a morning steamboat to Albany, and arranged for overnight lodging and board, they stepped outside and simply looked about them.

America. She really existed, they really stood on her soil, and no doubt her land really did stretch endlessly before them. But for Emilie, the arrival was bittersweet. Mama was not here. Karl was not here. Erich Jurgen was not here. Heidi had become a stranger.

"I must get a letter off to Meta," Papa declared suddenly. "The sooner it is sent, the sooner—" Emilie never heard the end of Papa's sentence, for Rosamund and Johanna Albrecht had come out of the octagonal building, crying. Herr Albrecht stood a few yards from them, looking so dejected his mustache sagged almost to his chin. Though a crowd was growing out here, too, his business partner was nowhere around.

"Lambert?" Both Papa and Reinhard Jurgen strode toward him. Emilie saw Rosamund catch sight of her, but the girl didn't shriek and stomp off. Her sobbing was too far gone into despair. The tiniest sliver of compassion nudged Emilie. Any condolence, though, would be attacked savagely. She watched.

Papa and Herr Jurgen came back looking grim. "The Albrechts' plans have changed, as we thought. We'll be on our way." But Papa was slow to move. A closed-mouth sigh escaped him.

Emilie heard the Jurgens' quiet, rapid exchange. When the two fathers then strolled a distance away, she approached

Frau Jurgen. "What's the matter?"

Frau Jurgen, cradling the baby, studied her. "I don't want to tempt you to gloat over Rosamund."

"Gloat?"

Frau Jurgen sighed. "But there's opportunity to learn here. I'm the one who warned how careful you and Rosamund would have to be about pride. 'Pride goeth before destruction and a haughty spirit before a fall.' Remember?"

Emilie nodded.

"Then maybe it's my responsibility to finish the lesson. Because your pride made Rosamund angry, you experienced a fall at her hands. Now she has had her own fall."

Emilie dearly wanted Frau Jurgen to go on. But she said, "I will pray not to gloat: That's just more pride. And that would bring another fall."

Frau Jurgen sighed again. "You will find out anyway. And there are safety reasons for telling you. The Albrechts won't be going with us tomorrow, Emilie."

Emilie wasn't at all sorry to hear this. Surely she could feel that way without rejoicing in Rosamund's trouble.

"That man we thought might have been Herr Albrecht's business partner? He was a con man. He picked Herr Albrecht out of the crowd as someone likely to have money, told him some phony investment story, and swindled him out of every *Pfennig* he had."

Aghast, Emilie cried, "You mean he was a runner?"

"Hush," Frau Jurgen cautioned. "Very like that, yes. Now, this must be a lesson to you: None of us is safe from such people until we reach Sheboygan, and maybe not even then. They will follow us, they know the language and we don't, and they are very clever. Anyone can be taken in. Anyone. Is that clear?" Solemnly, Emilie nodded.

"Unless Reinhard and your father can see a way to help them, the Albrechts will have to stay in New York."

"With—nothing?" Emilie couldn't help glancing at

Rosamund. The girl was mopping her face with a lace hand-kerchief.

"Oh, I wouldn't call it nothing." Frau Jurgen shifted Josef to her shoulder and rubbed his back. "They have their belongings. They have strong backs and hands to work. They have each other, if they will consider that a blessing. They have Hans and Dieter in Chicago who can send for them—at least I think so. It seems the business in Chicago may not be as prosperous as we've heard."

Papa and Herr Jurgen brushed past them, walking in Herr Albrecht's direction. As they passed, Emilie saw Herr Jurgen catch his wife's eye and shake his head.

Rosamund and Frau Albrecht waited, hankies and fingers twisted under their chins, for the news to be spoken: The Borners and Jurgens needed every *Taler* they had left just to put roofs over their families' heads for the winter. The Albrechts at least had a home waiting in Chicago. They would have to get there on their own.

"You know, the best help we can give them isn't money," Frau Jurgen murmured to Emilie as the Albrecht women collapsed in mourning. "It's to pray they find God. Without Him, even plenty can seem like nothing. But even those with nothing have something, if they have God."

Chapter Thirteen

Sheboygan, Wisconsin
October 20, 1855

My dearest friend, Louise,

Papa, Otto, and I landed here five days ago, all of us hale and hearty. We are staying at a place called Brown's Temperance Haus until Papa can buy land for what they call a farm. Farm is English for *Bauernhof.* Many hotels line the streets for us immigrants coming off the boats, but they are really just taverns with a few rooms to let. So we are here, where Deacon Brown doesn't allow drunkenness.

The weather is like home, and there are many pine trees, but I have never seen so much water in my life. Some Germans told Papa this is a very healthy state, no fever and ague or consumption like eastern America.

Sheboygan is wild but exciting. Boats full of Germans land every day, and people just spill onto the shore. Wagons are everywhere, some with big cloth roofs like bonnets, because that's how the Americans called Jankees get here from the east. Hogs graze in the public square. A runaway horse almost mowed me down yesterday. Rough-looking louts from a state called Ohio pull nets and nets full of white fish out of the lake. Peter, James, and John probably never saw so many fish. People don't like the sturgeon, so boys cut off their noses and use them for rubber balls! You can be sure Otto bounces fish noses all day long.

Dear friend, I'm sure by now Mama has come to you. I miss her, but I miss Karl, too. He said America would not be a land without sin, and he is right. These Jankees think we are ignorant and call us Dutchmen. People called Know Nothings accuse foreigners of stealing their jobs. Papa's friend, Herr Schulz, says there have been riots, and in another town even a lynching—by Germans! Some of the sin comes from our people, too.

But Karl could get a job easily, if he were here. Lots of cooper shops make barrels for all those fish to go to market in. Please tell him about the shops, if you see him.

Dear friend, I had to stop for awhile because Papa came in. He has bought farmland! So have the Jurgens! Papa will earn money by clearing away the trees and selling them to a sawmill, and he will build us a log cabin before the snow flies. I am too excited to write any more.

I remain your dearest friend in all the world,
Emilie Borner.

* * *

"How big is the farm, Papa?"

Papa sat at the desk in their spartan room at Brown's Temperance House, about to write to Mama. "Eighty acres," he answered. "That's 128 *Morgen* or so."

Emilie gasped. The farm in Thuringen had been only a few *Morgen* in area. "So much? Then we are rich!"

Papa smiled. "Yes and no. Yes, because anyone God provides for is rich indeed. I was able to buy for the lowest price allowed by law—one and a quarter dollars per acre! That's one hundred American dollars or about 140 *Talers*."

"For a whole farm?" cried Emilie.

Papa nodded. "I want your brother to hear this too. Otto!"

he called through the open window.

Otto, juggling sturgeon noses, appeared quickly.

"Our land," said Papa, "is in section sixteen of the town of Mosel. Section sixteen is always state land, not federal, because it's designated for the use of schools."

Emilie followed his meaning. "We will be living near a school?"

"That's my hope, yes."

"Will we go right away?" asked Otto. "To school, I mean?"

"Well, no." Papa's face clouded, though Otto couldn't hide a smile. "When your sister got it in mind that we're rich, I told her yes and no."

Emilie had forgotten all about the no part.

"The truth is, we'll need a full day's work from all of us, six days a week. Buying the farm has taken everything we had left, even the money for next week's keep here." Papa paused. "How I wish Karl had come. He could have gotten into a cooper shop the first day."

There was a pensive silence.

"But—God be praised. I wasn't sure we could afford land at all, yet we have. The weather is good, and I've found us a wagon ride. We leave after the noon meal." Dismissing them, Papa turned to the desk, pen scratching busily across the paper.

That afternoon they were on the final leg of their journey to their new home.

* * *

"Are we to sleep out in the open?" Emilie whispered to Frau Jurgen. The Borners, Jurgens, Papa's friend Heinrich Schulz, and other neighbors had gathered on the Borners' property, which was simply land covered with trees and brush. Red and gold leaves rained everywhere.

"By tomorrow you will have a makeshift camp like we have," replied Frau Jurgen. "Tonight, the Zimmermanns will take you home. We stayed there last night. They are wonderful, generous believers who lodge newcomers most every day."

Conversation faded as the music of axes and saws sang on the wind. Trees began to topple, the pale wood exposed by the cuts looking raw and vulnerable. While one man hitched up oxen to drive logs to the sawmill for sale, others shoved logs aside to serve as poles for the lean-to. The straightest and strongest logs were rolled by more borrowed oxen to the site Papa had chosen for the cabin.

Frau Jurgen and Emilie led Josef and Heidi well away from the falling timber. A stout woman in a babushka, Frau Zimmermann grinned at Emilie. "Welcome to your first logging bee."

Frau Jurgen smiled. "I see how this works. Whenever a new farm is started, neighbors come in and share the labor."

"And not only for the logging," said Frau Zimmermann. "For the raising, and the housewarming dance. And for years after, the quilting bees, the spinning bees, the sugaring bees, the stump-pulling bees. All with merrymaking and plenty of food." Frau Zimmermann surveyed her two companions. "*Ach*, you got thin in the old country. You will get plump here, just see if you don't."

Leaving the two women talking, Emilie strolled a short distance away where Heidi sat propped against a tree. The little girl had scooped leaves into her lap, and she tossed them up and watched them drift down, over and over.

"I see your new teeth are all grown in," Emilie said.

Heidi kept tossing leaves.

"Did you have a bumpy ride out to your new farm?" She joined Heidi on the ground. "The roads are so bad here I thought *my* teeth would shake loose!"

"It was fun at first," Heidi said. "I bounced and jiggled all over. Then I bit my tongue. And Josef cried."

Encouraged, Emilie said carefully, "Josef will be blessed to grow up with a big sister like you. You've always known how to have fun."

Heidi stirred her leaves harder. She began pushing them toward Emilie, then flinging armloads. Rising up on her knees, Emilie batted them back.

"I'm glad we aren't on a boat anymore," Heidi said. After several more volleys of leaves she added, "You are still my favorite Emilie."

Emilie's heart soared. She longed to tell Heidi what an answer to prayer this was, but she stopped herself. She rolled Heidi in leaves and stuck them in her hair. By the time Papa called her to gather brush for the shelter, Heidi was giggling.

* * *

At dusk, the Zimmermanns took the Borners home in their wagon. "In a few days you'll have a cabin very like this," Frau Zimmermann told Emilie as they entered the house.

The Zimmermanns' one-room cabin had a floor of rough, uneven planks. Next to numerous wall pegs where trousers and jackets hung, a ladder of split logs and saplings rose to a loft under the roof.

"Children sleep up there, usually," Frau Zimmermann said. "Our girls sleep on the trundle bed, though. We save the loft for guests."

Emilie nodded, but her eyes slid away from the woman to wander.

"That's it, feel free to look around. You can see a little of how things go." Frau Zimmermann bustled to the fireplace, which was stone and covered one entire end of the house. Taking up what looked like a huge bird's wing, she brushed the hearth. "A clean hearth is a clean room." She then plunked several logs onto the fire and poked it up to a roar. Last, she heaved a huge kettle onto the iron crane and swung it over the flames.

The fire warmed the room, and the aroma of vegetable soup quickly filled it. As Frau Zimmermann dropped dumpling batter into the kettle, Emilie approached. "I wasn't sure I'd ever smell something this good again."

"*Ach*, they all say that, and don't I love hearing it." The

98

woman beamed. "Your brother misses sauerkraut, if I hear right. We have that too, and some good rye bread. Rye isn't so easy to come by here. Americans eat nothing but white." Emptying her dumpling bowl, Frau Zimmermann clapped the lid back onto the soup kettle. "Like so. Cooking over a fire takes getting used to. I'll have a cookstove soon, and you'll want one too, soon as your papa can get you one."

Apprehension swam in Emilie. But just then a tall, freckled girl came in. Slimmer than Frau Zimmermann, the girl looked much like her, even wearing the same loose blouse and white apron.

"Hilda, take Emilie outside, to see the yard and the oven and such. She needs to know how we do here."

"Yes, Mama." Hilda's voice was sweet but prim. She led Emilie out to the rear of the cabin. "Here is the oven. Mama claims the bread is sweeter and more wholesome baked outside."

Emilie gazed at the large stone oven. It was much like the fireplace except that it had a door.

"We're blessed to have an oven of our own, but those who don't are welcome to share ours. You can too, till your papa builds you one."

Emilie swallowed.

"And here's the ash hopper." Emilie strained to see the V-shaped structure through growing darkness. "Every home has this. But you know about making soap from lye, don't you?"

Emilie nodded slowly.

"And we have the smokehouse, for curing meat and sausage. We eat mostly wild game. Papa goes out hunting, but sometimes he just stands in the doorway and shoots deer that run past."

"You mean—food runs past your door?"

"Unheard of, isn't it, for people who've gone through the crop failures at home? But this is no Eden. Last year we got all done planting a wheat field and the passenger pigeons came. It was eerie; they darkened the sun and their wings beat like a windstorm. They dived to the ground and picked the field clean of seed in five minutes. Papa shot about fifty of them, and it made no difference at all."

Emilie wasn't sure what to say. "You've learned a lot about living in Wisconsin."

"You will too. The hard work is less in vain than in Germany. You have a chance at your share of the bounty."

Even when birds eat your seed? Emilie felt hollow. "Mama should have come." She barely knew she was speaking aloud. "She only wanted a fair chance to earn a living."

Hilda sighed. "Often some of the family stays behind. That's not so strange. But since she didn't come, the woman's work will fall to you."

Emilie met Hilda's eyes: clear, gray, matter-of-fact. "I know how to work."

Hilda nodded. "I'm sure you do, and it's a good thing. Because in a new country like America, you work or die."

Chapter Fourteen

Emilie helped her family and neighbors build two cabins, one each for the Borners and the Jurgens.

From sunup to sundown, trees were felled, rolled, notched, and lifted into place atop the growing walls. Emilie and Heidi raced Otto to dig clay or gather moss to plug the chinks between the logs. At other times Emilie drove a wagon back to the Zimmermanns' to help pick the last of the apples from the orchard for *Apfelkuchen*, or to lift loaves to or from the stone oven with long-handled paddles. With the hot food carefully wrapped, she would then drive back to the building site and serve the workers.

If the weather grew more autumn-like in late October, Emilie barely noticed. The sun and hard work gave her skin a constant sheen, as well as her muscles a noticeable ache. At night, while Papa still worked splitting logs into shingles by candlelight, she would roll up in a woolen blanket under the camp's brush roof and sleep. Only twice did she wake early, once dampened with rain, the other time sung to by wolves until dawn.

Finally, moving-in day came for the Borners. The cabin roof, built of hollowed-out logs to shed rain, was finished. The windows had been cut into the walls; the stone fireplace and chimney were ready. The door, though, wasn't quite right. Before it could be hung, its opening would have to be enlarged.

"I'm so glad for you," Frau Jurgen told Emilie, as they cleared away the remains of the noon meal. "Now that we all have our heads under a proper roof, why—"

A scream—a man's scream—pierced the air. In the cabin doorway, a crowd leaned over a slumped figure. Feet pounding, Emilie and Frau Jurgen ran to see.

"Heinrich!"

"Saw . . ." groaned the injured man. "Slipped . . ."

"Cut the leg off his pants," ordered a terse voice.

Reaching the scene of the accident, Emilie gasped. Herr Schulz's left leg was gashed. A ribbon of blood seeped along the slit in his trousers, the loose threads soaking it up like millions of tiny wicks.

"Who's got a wad of tobacco?" hollered a man.

"Spider webs are what you want. A ball of them stuffed into a wound stops bleeding."

"*Ach*, where do we get spider webs off a brand-new cabin?"

"If Franz Borner weren't a temperance man, I'd have my little brown jug here to wash that out good."

Then Papa and Reinhard Jurgen jumped into the fray, Papa with prayer and Herr Jurgen with torn strips of shirt to wind around the cut. As Herr Schulz was helped into a wagon to be driven home, a quiet descended on the settlers.

"Praise God it didn't hit a blood vessel."

"Sliced to the bone, though."

"As long as infection doesn't set in . . ."

"He'll be off his feet awhile. He'll be needing help, that's for sure."

Abruptly, another neighbor moved to the doorway and took Herr Schulz's place.

"Should we call off the housewarming?" Emilie asked Frau Zimmermann and Della Jurgen.

"Not at all," asserted Frau Zimmermann. "Look, the musicians are going to warm up already." Two men passed through the door, one with an instrument case and the other with a concertina. "Gottlieb Graf has his mouth organ too, just see if he doesn't. Accidents are a fact of life here." Frau Zimmermann shook her head. "We wish Heinrich well, but everything moves along. Come, girl, I'll help you lay your cabin's first fire. I have a special gift, too." The plump woman smiled.

Emilie entered the cabin. She felt a little thrill when Papa "closed" the door behind her by fitting it into its frame and beginning to hang it. The chatter and laughter of friends and neighbors warmed her, even before the firewood caught flame and heat radiated into the room.

"Now, the gift." Frau Zimmermann proudly handed Emilie a package, loosely wrapped in plain paper and tied with string. "Undo it carefully." Emilie eased the wrapping off to find a fold of feathers like the one Frau Zimmermann used to sweep her hearth.

"Your own turkey wing. A clean hearth is a clean room."

Emilie smiled, although something seemed to settle about her shoulders. She suspected "something" was named Responsibility. "Thank you, Frau Zimmermann."

The musicians started playing immediately, and neighbors began to dance, clap, and sing. "If we can still carry on like this after working so hard, I guess we're not so old after all," Frau Zimmermann remarked.

"Tough luck if we are," said Frau Graf, wife of the mouth-organ player. "Frontier life is not for the infirm."

"Rather than bemoan tough luck," chimed in another, "pray Heinrich Schulz is not among the infirm after today."

Troubled, Emilie stepped away from the group. She'd been ready to join the singing, to coax Heidi into a dance, but suddenly she was afraid. With one wrong slip of a tool, a strapping family man had become an invalid. However would she manage, keeping house alone in a new, wild country? How would her family cope if something happened to her?

"Emilie?" Frau Jurgen, holding Josef, spoke softly beside her. "Is it Herr Schulz you're thinking of?"

Emilie turned to her friend. "No," she said earnestly, "it's me." She drew a breath. "And it's strange to have a party without Mama and Karl here. Merrymaking on the ship was different. It wasn't actually our home."

Frau Jurgen nodded. "I know, Emilie. Erich's bed waits in

our loft, and I don't know if that makes things easier or harder. With new homes built, we feel even more that we've gone on without our loved ones."

Emilie's gaze wandered to the built-in bed, its frame strung with a web of ropes holding the feather mattress. It was a double bed. Whether Mama's half would be empty for always, she couldn't bear to think. Was the future in Wisconsin really any surer than in Germany? It seemed shrouded in fog.

Frau Jurgen's hand crept onto Emilie's shoulder. "God doesn't reward our trust by leading us astray. Scripture gives us every right, and even a duty, to hope."

Emilie nodded. She needed to hope. "I'm going to find Heidi and ask if she'd like to dance."

Heidi, giggling, did take a few spins on the plank floor. Hilda Zimmermann danced shyly with a young man of about twenty. "They'll marry soon," another girl confided to Emilie. "Everyone knows it."

These moments of good cheer were short. Just as Emilie was about to dance a *Schottische* with Heidi, Frau Zimmermann spoke a few innocent words that turned the party upside down.

"Emilie." She bustled over to the young people. "We've got bread, pickles, pretzels, cherries, and plates and forks for everything except the *Kuchen.* Do you have plates we could use to serve the *Kuchen?*"

Emilie understood in a flash that Mama would offer the lusterware. What she didn't understand was why Heidi's shoulders stiffened under her hand. "Yes, Frau Zimmermann. I can unpack them easily."

Heidi fled.

"Heidi? I won't be long," Emilie called, but she knew Heidi wouldn't listen. She remembered how Heidi had played with the trunk latches on the ship and at the immigration station. Was she afraid of trunks, of their yawning mouths and dark insides, perhaps? Had she been assuring herself that the latches were fastened down tight?

"Your dishes seem to unnerve her somehow," Heidi's mother said, coming to help.

"Maybe it's good if I unpack them and store that trunk out of sight," Emilie agreed. They eased the trunk over the rough flooring, away from the dancing feet, and unsnapped the latches.

"I think the dessert plates are on the sides, on top of the dinner plates," Emilie said. She lifted newspaper and burlap from the top and picked up a cloth-wrapped plate. But something in the package shifted. One side of the cloth sagged too low. Emilie unwrapped the plate hurriedly.

"It's broken!" she cried, holding up two halves.

"This one, too." Frau Jurgen showed her a plate that appeared to have been bitten into.

Emilie sagged back on her heels. "No wonder they say not to bring china." She pulled plate after plate from the chest, pulled off the wrappings, then started on pieces from the middle so they wouldn't topple: sugar bowl, gravy boat, cups. Those that weren't shattered were at least badly chipped.

"Here, Frau Zimmermann can put *Kuchen* on these." Emilie handed dishes to Hilda. "But we'll never use them again, will we? Unless we get desperately poor." Perhaps, she thought, they were desperately poor already.

"I'm sorry, Emilie," Frau Jurgen said gently. "I wonder if Heidi knew they had broken, and was worried we'd be angry?" She shook her head. "No, that makes no sense."

Emilie felt her eyes brimming.

"Emilie?"

"They're Karl's inheritance." Her throat worked. "Karl's inheritance is smashed."

"And one of his ties to the New World is smashed, too?" Frau Jurgen ventured.

Emilie's tears dribbled over.

Frau Jurgen wrenched the trunk aside and led Emilie out into the autumn dusk. "I don't want you to take this as a sign from God that Karl doesn't belong here."

"But what if he doesn't?" Emilie sobbed. "And if he doesn't come, Mama never will either."

"Oh, Emilie, I don't know. I can't pretend I do." Frau Jurgen put her arm around Emilie's shoulders and hugged tight. "I ask God to plant a desire in everyone's hearts to follow His way more than their own. I ask God to guide us through whatever comes."

Emilie sniffled. "Those are good things to pray."

"That part about following God's way more than our own? That's for us, too, not just Karl and Erich."

"It is?"

Frau Jurgen nodded. "Should God wish to leave them in Germany, it will be up to us to accept it. I remind myself often of His promise that all things work together for good when we love God and are called according to His purpose. Do you know that Scripture?"

"Romans 8:28. Papa reads it all the time now," Emilie said. "But I don't know if I understand it. Maybe I never did."

"God can see inside our hearts," Frau Jurgen said. "If we obey Him, and want to fulfill His purpose for us, He promises all things work out for good."

Emilie shivered in the chill air. "Like Meta coming over on Mama's ticket. But I don't see how Mama being left in Germany can be good."

"Maybe it isn't," said Frau Jurgen. "The verse says all things work together for good, not that each thing that happens is good in itself, or seems good right away."

Emilie pondered this.

"We might as well finish unpacking your dishes, and let your papa know what's happened if he doesn't already."

More cups and saucers came out of the chest, chipped and cracked. Emilie and Della Jurgen unwrapped every bundle as carefully as they would baby Josef, yet each one yielded disappointing shards of shiny copper and blue. People looked over their shoulders.

"Pity. You know what they say about bringing china."

"It's a shame, but dishes can be had in Sheboygan."

Emilie picked up the loose wrapping that she knew contained the cream pitcher. No hope for this piece. None at all.

She opened it—and gasped. Surprise made her let go, and it skidded down her lap.

"Oh!" Frau Jurgen caught the pitcher and lifted it. "Emilie! It's whole, and—"Whatever else she meant to say died on her lips.

The lusterware cream pitcher was stuffed with paper money.

Chapter Fifteen

Frau Jurgen clasped the pitcher to her bosom. "Your mama must have put it here for safekeeping—what a blessing!" Frau Jurgen replaced the pitcher in the trunk and covered it. "Speak to your papa about it later. Oh, Emilie," she whispered happily, "God provides in such unexpected ways."

Stunned, Emilie rejoined the party but barely heard the music and laughter. Had God really provided for their winter needs through Mama? She thought back to the farewell party in August, when she and Louise had moved the trunk into the pantry.

She had unwrapped the cream pitcher to show Louise. Of course it had been empty then. Heidi had appeared suddenly, and Emilie had covered the pitcher hastily and closed the trunk. Later, she and Louise had seen the chest moved out of place, had added more cloth and newspapers over the dishes, and fastened the latches. Emilie was sure that when she'd opened the trunk today, it had looked just the way she'd left it.

The money must have been placed in the pitcher after she'd shown it to Louise, but before they'd closed the chest for the last time.

Rosamund Albrecht would never have stashed money in the Borners' china. That idea was laughable. And had Rosamund snooped in the chest and *found* the cash, she might well have stolen it. Absently, Emilie shook her head. At least three people had been in the trunk the day of the party. It was too hard to believe there were more. Rosamund had not been in the trunk at all.

But Mama hadn't, either. Had Mama hidden funds in the cream pitcher, she would not have left it so clumsily wrapped.

*   *   *

All evening, Emilie's head spun with possible names of the money stasher—Papa himself? Karl? Had Karl crept into her room in Bremen to get the money back? But why even put it there? It made no sense.

Strangely, with Emilie's silence, Heidi had grown livelier. "Dance with me, my favorite Emilie," she'd chirped. "Do the *Vogelsong.* Let's go outside." Finally, only the Borners and Jurgens were left at the new cabin. With Heidi distracted by some silliness from Otto, Emilie could wait no longer. Almost pulling Papa along, she opened the china trunk, took out the pitcher, and tipped it so he could look inside.

Papa lost his breath. "Speaking of treasure in earthen vessels," he managed. He eased the money out and slowly leafed through it.

"It's a surprise to you, too."

Papa gazed. "How many people know about this?"

"Only Frau Jurgen. It's just that I've been wondering who could have put it there, and it couldn't have been anybody."

They stared at each other.

"Frau Jurgen says God blessed us," Emilie told Papa.

"I have no other explanation," Papa returned. "Reinhard," he called. Both Herr and Frau Jurgen came over. Otto and Heidi followed. "It was in the dishes." Papa opened his palm.

Heidi burst into tears and collapsed on the floor.

"Heidi!" exclaimed both Emilie and Della Jurgen.

"Jesus isn't real! He's not! That Bible verse is wrong."

"What Bible verse?" Frau Jurgen handed Josef to her husband and gathered Heidi onto her lap. "What Bible verse is wrong, Heidi?"

"That one about your treasure and your heart being in the same place."

Emilie had a vague memory of what Heidi meant. But before she could think back, Herr Jurgen recited the verse: "'For where your treasure is, there will your heart be also.'"

"You read us that verse, Papa, the day we went to the party at Emilie's farm." Heidi's tone was almost accusing, and she looked suddenly afraid.

"Heidi," Frau Jurgen began quietly. "Whose treasure and heart are in separate places now?"

"Erich's!" sobbed the child.

"And Erich is in Germany . . . so his money is here? This is Erich's money?"

Emilie's mouth fell open.

Heidi folded her arms over her head and rocked. "I'm sorry! I'm sorry!"

"Heidi," said Reinhard Jurgen. "You'd better tell us what you've done."

"I heard Erich tell Karl he'd only pretend to go to America, then sneak away. But he'd need the money he saved. And that verse said your money and your heart stay together. So I—" Heidi looked stricken.

"You sent Erich's money to America, so he would come too?" her father asked.

Heidi nodded miserably.

"You stole it?"

"Not to keep," Heidi wailed. "To pack in something that was going to America. But when I found the money and hid it in my pocket, Mama said it was time to hurry to Emilie's for the party. It was still in my pocket when we got there, and I didn't want to lose it." Heidi paused. "I saw Emilie and Louise looking at the china, all packed up for America. When they went away, I put Erich's money in a dish."

"In the pitcher," Emilie said softly, "because I'd left the wrapping loose."

Heidi nodded.

"Heidi, when your mama and I opened the trunk a little while ago, you were afraid we'd find the money, weren't you?"

More nodding.

"Then, when we didn't say anything about it, did you

think it must not be there anymore?"

Still more nodding.

"So you felt better, because it might mean God had sent the money back to Erich? So God might be real after all?"

Heidi's head was almost in her lap now, still nodding.

"And several times you wanted to check the china trunk, on the ship and after we got off, to see if the money might be gone and you could feel better."

Every eye other than Heidi's watched Emilie in amazement. Heidi nodded.

Reinhard Jurgen let his breath out hard. "I wonder at what point in his wanderings my son discovered he was penniless." He focused on Heidi. "Stealing is wrong."

"I know, Papa. I'm sorry. It didn't work, either," Heidi mourned. "Jesus didn't bring Erich to America with his money."

"Oh, Heidi, the verse doesn't mean you can never be parted from your money," Frau Jurgen crooned. "It means— whatever is worth most to us, that's what we love the best."

Heidi stared into space. "It does?" she finally asked.

"What happened to you doesn't mean Jesus isn't real, *Liebchen*. It means you didn't quite understand the verse. That happens to everyone. Big people, too. All the time."

"It does?" Heidi nibbled a finger.

"Do you believe stealing is wrong?" came her papa's deep voice.

Heidi nodded again. "I'm sorry, Papa."

"Well, it's God's law that tells us when we're wrong." The softness of Herr Jurgen's rumble fascinated Emilie. "So, you see, Heidi, you do believe God is real, after all."

*   *   *

Days of hard work passed as the last of the leaves fell and the sky turned gray. Papa, Herr Jurgen, and other neighbors shared tools and labor to dig wells, then Papa chose a spot for the first garden and cleared trees from it. Emilie and Otto gathered brush into great heaps for burning. After the fire, they spread ashes over the garden area for fertilizer. The smell of burning brush and leaves hung in the air night and day.

Little by little, Papa and Otto built furniture: three-legged stools, a trundle bed, a table and chairs. Papa hunted deer and small animals for food, then taught Emilie. The day she shot a squirrel, Papa was almost happier than she. Only on Sundays did the work stop for church, visiting, and amusements. With his first income from logging and shingle-making, Papa bought winter coats, a team of oxen, and a wagon.

"We can't build a barn yet, maybe next year," Papa told Otto and Emilie. It was late November, and they were eating a supper of rabbit along with fruits and nuts from the forest.

Emilie's mind was not on barns, but on the rabbit. Uncertain how to cook it, she had simply browned the meat in a kettle and simmered it until tender. She had spent a lot of time adjusting the pot over the fire. Was it too close? Too far away? In the end, the rabbit was only slightly charred.

"Emilie, this is a fine meal," Papa praised. Otto rolled his eyes and briefly pantomimed choking, but he ate everything.

"Is it really all right?" Emilie was sure Papa would eat her cooking and demand that Otto do the same no matter how bad it was.

"Indeed. Better a bit blackened than raw." He changed the subject back to outdoor work. "We'll let up on the logging some till winter and early spring. Those are really the best times to clear land. What we'll do next is build the oxen a shelter of poles and straw. Many Jankees let their livestock wander all winter, Herr Schulz says, and forage for themselves. But that's no way to do."

"Papa," Otto said. "Didn't you plan to sell logs steady to the sawmill?"

"Well, that brings me to my news."

"News?" Emilie looked up quickly. "A letter from Mama?"

Papa looked amazed. "No, Emilie. What would a letter from Mama have to do with logs?"

Chastened, Emilie apologized for interrupting.

"It's too soon yet for a letter. It's been barely seven weeks since I posted the first one from New York. Letters have to go all the way to Germany, then the person has to write back, then the letter has to travel all the way here."

"Yes, Papa," Emilie said because she knew Papa wanted to say something. But why would Mama wait for a letter from them? Why couldn't she just send one in care of Herr Schulz, as they'd written to her in care of the Conrads? Emilie was sure a letter could reach them any day.

"Emilie?" Papa said. "Were you listening?"

Emilie jerked to attention.

"I was explaining how we could afford to ease up on logging for a month or so. Herr Schulz, being laid up, needs to hire farm help. Otto will help with the children's work: feeding stock, milking the cow, fetching in wood, churning, since their girl is too small to do it all. Frau Schulz has to get the last of the harvest in, as well as do the cooking and the washing and the nursing of her husband."

Emilie nodded.

"So God has made good use of your employment with the Blumenfelds, even if it seemed to turn out badly."

Emilie felt confused, yet the Bible verse about things working together for good ran through her mind. "I don't understand, Papa."

"Starting tomorrow you have a job at the Schulz farm, minding the baby."

Chapter Sixteen

Emilie knew little about babies, and didn't see how reading to the Blumenfeld children had prepared her. Eight-month-old Arno Schulz was cheerful, but plump and squealing as a piglet and nearly as fast.

"Arno, hot!" Emilie would yelp as the baby streaked toward the fireplace on all fours. "Arno, you'll get splinters," she exclaimed when he rubbed his hands on the rungs of the ladder. "Arno, not in your mouth," she cried when Arno found a thimble between the floorboards. At least the Schulzes wouldn't test her honesty with money, she thought. They didn't dare leave any lying around.

The second week of December, snow flew. Emilie took care of Arno while Frau Schulz caught up on the washing and baking and spinning and candle making.

Herr Schulz, seldom stirring from bed, told stories of pioneers overcoming blizzards and rescuing pigs from bears. Playing pat-a-cake with Arno and singing the *Vogelsong* with little Frieda, Emilie noticed Frau Schulz spending more and more time unwrapping her husband's leg, salving it, and bandaging it up again. Once Emilie saw the cut—puffy, red, and draining. Herr Schulz's leg was infected.

Flurries continued. The logs of the Borners' cabin had shrunk, and whistling of wind through the cracks now accompanied the nightly howling of beasts. Tired as she was, Emilie lay awake in her loft feeling utterly alone.

What was Mama doing tonight? Or Karl? Or Louise? Surely not tossing firebrands among the wolf packs that bayed at their door. The total change in her life made her feel so apart from people in Germany.

Emilie awoke on her thirteenth birthday, December 13, to the sight of frosty white mounds clinging to the inside corners of the cabin. But to her amazement only patchy snow gleamed under fluffy clouds and flickering sun.

"Today's the day," Papa said at breakfast. Emilie looked up in surprise. Mama wasn't here to bake something special, or give her a gift such as hair ribbons or new stockings. Was Papa going to do something for her birthday?

"Today's the day we start logging again?" Otto asked.

"No." Papa buttered a biscuit. "Though it would be a smart day for it."

Today's the day we hear from Mama? Emilie made herself keep quiet. Papa wouldn't know such a thing so early in the morning. But she couldn't help hoping. Today was her birthday, and Emilie Katharina Christina Borner had been born hoping.

"Today's the day I take Heinrich into Sheboygan," Papa said, "even if I have to truss him like a turkey and load him in the wagon. Without a doctor, or at least some decent treatment for that leg, he's going to lose it.

"I chopped firewood, so you should have plenty. I'll be gone one night, two at most. And when I get back," Papa paused and smiled, "I'll try to have a little something for my girl's birthday."

* * *

Squaring his shoulders importantly, Otto started hauling in wood almost before Papa and the wagon had disappeared. "What are you cooking today?"

"Well, we have some venison," Emilie said, getting into the spirit of being on their own. "And I should mix some bread dough and walk over to the Zimmermanns' to bake it."

Otto shook his head solemnly. "Better stick to a pan over the fire. Clouds are rolling in."

Emilie laughed. "You will make a marvelous papa someday, but will you ever give up bouncing sturgeon noses? That is the question."

"Emilie, I'm not joking. Look outside."

The cabin did seem gloomier. Emilie went to the door and threw it open. The sun had gone out like a candle. The blue spaces in the sky had been filled in by clouds as thick as sheep's wool. Snowflakes began to dance in the air. "Otto?" Emilie said. "Let's get in more firewood."

Staggering back and forth with all they could carry, they brought in only half the wood before the screaming wind and snow blinded them. Emilie slammed the door and moaned, "This is one of those blizzards Herr Schulz talks about. How will Papa make it to Sheboygan?"

"Well, he'll probably have an adventure," Otto said. "Herr Schulz told me a story about a man whose cow wandered away in a blizzard. He got lost in the woods leading it home, so he tied it to a tree while he figured out where he was. Did you hear this one?"

Emilie shook her head. Otto continued. "When the man went back to get the cow, he found it had pulled the rope so tight he couldn't undo the knot. He didn't have a knife, so he tried to shoot the rope apart. But he missed and killed the cow."

Emilie couldn't help laughing. "Otto!" she exclaimed. "You'd better hope Papa doesn't shoot one of the oxen. And how could he, since they are hitched to the wagon and can't wander off?"

"And how could he," Otto echoed, "when the gun is right here?"

Emilie's gaze went to the gun, hanging on hooks over the door. "Maybe they have Herr Schulz's. Let's poke up the fire." She added two logs, carefully placing them between the backlog, which kept smoke out of the cabin, and the forestick, which kept burning logs from tumbling into the room. Flames leaped up.

"Your turn to tell a story from Herr Schulz," Otto said.

Emilie scraped a three-legged stool closer to the fire and picked up her knitting. She was not about to tell a story of a man caught in a blizzard, whose frozen body was found hugging a fence post, all because he'd gone out to buy an ax handle in perfectly fine weather. "Otto, most of Herr Schulz's stories are not very comforting."

"I don't want comfort. I want adventure."

"Well, all right." Emilie made a few more stitches on a scarf for Papa while she thought. "There was a family who had no flour. The man had to go away on business, and on his way he stopped to order some. The miller promised to send a sack of flour to the man's family, but—"

"But what?"

Emilie reluctantly went on. "A blizzard came up and the flour didn't get there. The man traveled in the opposite direction and didn't know this, and meanwhile his family lived for a week on only salt pork and wild onions."

Otto was silent for a few moments. "What happened at the end of the week?"

"The father headed back, picked up another sack of flour on his way, and took it home."

"So then they had flour."

"Yes."

"And everything was all right."

"Yes."

"Tell another one."

"Your turn."

"Well," said Otto, "a man and his wife—" He paused, and they listened to the wind whistle. "It's not stopping, is it?"

"It's coming through the chinks, Otto."

They watched the tiny whirlwinds of snow that played near the inside walls. Snow rounded the cabin's inner corners all the way to the ceiling.

"Well," Otto repeated, "a man and his wife lived all winter on nothing but flour. In spring—"

"Wait," said Emilie. "Nothing but flour? Not even a little lard or yeast to mix with it?" Germany hadn't been that bad.

"Nothing but flour. So in spring, the man made thirty-five kilograms of maple sugar. He carried it on his back to Milwaukee, sold it to buy supplies, and carried those home on his back with five cents left over. But he was too tired to make it."

"What happened?" Emilie asked warily. No doubt he'd say a blizzard blew up.

"The man stopped at a cabin and asked for three cents' worth of bread. When the family heard his story, they gave him a whole meal free."

Emilie knitted several stitches without speaking. "I was wrong, Otto," she said. "Most of Herr Schulz's stories *are* comforting. They tell how situations that could have killed people turned out right."

It was Otto's turn to be quiet. "You think maybe that's why he told those stories? So he could feel like his leg might be all right too?"

Emilie set down her knitting. "Otto, we have something to hope in that's better than stories. We need to pray for Papa and Herr Schulz." She glanced around, listening to the wind. Only this log box of a cabin kept the blizzard from swallowing them. "And for ourselves."

Chapter Seventeen

The instant Emilie said "Amen," Otto shot to the door and yanked it open. Snow tumbled into the room.

"Otto, what are you doing?" Emilie shrieked. The air was white, the world blank.

"We don't want to get trapped inside." Otto grabbed the shovel that stood beside the door and began heaving snow away from the opening. Had there been another shovel, Emilie would have joined him. As it was, she simply watched him work, filled with an odd hope even now. *God, it's as if You spoke to him, telling him what to do.*

For their meal they had venison and pancakes, but Emilie was dismayed by the tiny food supply. "Lord, we trust You to feed us, as You fed the crowd with five loaves and two fish," she prayed.

"Why did you say that?" Otto asked suspiciously.

"We're going to have to be careful," Emilie said. "The venison is gone. We don't have much flour, either, and no yeast. I couldn't have gone to the Zimmermanns' to bake anyway." She giggled nervously, thinking of Herr Schulz's stories.

"What else have we got?"

"Berries and hickory nuts."

"Well, then. We're fine."

Emilie stared at him. "The berries and nuts will go fast, if that's all we have. Why do you think I prayed the way I did?"

"If God's going to multiply our food, why worry?"

"Otto Borner," Emilie thundered. "We can't ask God to do a miracle just so we can eat like pigs. We'll eat only when we're hungry. We'll have to ration."

Otto scowled and didn't speak through several mouthfuls, then said, "Papa probably means to bring supplies back from Sheboygan."

"He probably does."

"It could—be a long time before he gets back, couldn't it? Since the storm started on his way there?"

"Yes," Emilie said. "He wouldn't turn back, because of Herr Schulz's leg. And once they make it to town, they'll be stranded there until the snow stops."

While Emilie cleaned up after the meal, Otto opened the door again and shoveled a space around the entrance. Emilie put wood on the fire, frowning at the woodpile. Already it was growing smaller. They went to bed early, to make the night pass faster. Emilie was just drifting to sleep when she remembered again that today had been her birthday.

*　*　*

Two nights passed—the two nights Papa said he'd be gone—and still it snowed. The temperature plummeted. Midday on December 15, the wood in the house ran out.

"We've got to go out to the woodpile," said Otto. "There's as much out there as we had in here, if only we can get it."

"But what about Herr Schulz's stories?" argued Emilie, knitting on Papa's scarf. "That one about a man who . . ."

"Well, finish up. A man who what?"

"Froze to death in a whiteout because he missed his house by four feet."

"Did you want to freeze to death in here without trying to help ourselves? That's a lot more stupid."

Of course he was right. "The wood will be buried in snow," Emilie said.

"Yes, but at least I can get out the door. Maybe I can shovel the pile clear." He ran for the door, and Emilie nearly tackled him. "I need my coat, right?"

"And mittens, and scarf. And you need something I learned from Herr Schulz's stories." Emilie put on her own coat, fetched a rope, and tied it to a loop on Otto's trousers. "I am going to hold onto the other end of this. If you get lost out there, I will reel you in like a fish. Understand?"

A grin flashed across Otto's face. "Just don't cut off my nose and bounce it, all right?"

Emilie laughed in spite of herself. Armed with the shovel, Otto opened the door, trailing a long tail of rope behind him.

It seemed as if he took forever. Emilie wondered if her own frozen body would be discovered in the doorway, holding a rope that snaked out into nothingness. She fretted that the rope was so long she couldn't tell what was happening on Otto's end. What if, with his struggle to get wood, the rope had dropped off his pants? Emilie fought down panic, then tensed. Had she heard a cry?

"Emilie!"

She had! She began to wind the rope around her hand. Finally she felt weight on the rope, and indeed reeled her brother in, backward. He dropped three logs at her feet.

"Again," Otto puffed. "The same way. I can't turn and follow the rope back. I can't see it."

Emilie checked the knot on Otto's end of the rope and sent him out again six more times. They piled the wood near the fireplace, stoked the fire, and fell in front of it, freezing and exhausted.

*　　*　　*

Another night passed. The cabin, never toasty warm, was frigid after they'd held the door open so long. Emilie and Otto gave up their beds to doze fitfully in front of the fire, jumping up to feed it logs and keep it roaring. The wood supply dwindled.

"Otto," Emilie said quietly, heating a mixture of lard and flour over the fire. "I've prayed a blessing over this, that maybe it will turn out something like biscuit crumbs. This is the end of the flour. It's gone."

"So we have just nuts and berries?"

Emilie nodded.

Otto spoke words she herself had thought. "We weren't this poor in Germany."

"Frau Jurgen told me something on the ship," Emilie said, almost dreamlike. "She said whatever happened to me, to remember I'm a king's child."

"Was it a mistake to come to America?" Otto asked. "Was Karl right?"

Emilie shook her head. To answer any other way would crush their spirits. "Do you believe in Jesus, Otto?"

Otto stared. "You know I do! I got in trouble for standing up to Frau Albrecht on the ship. Remember?"

"Then you're a king's child, too, and the King will take care of us." Wrapped in her blanket, Emilie scurried away from the fire long enough to grab Papa's Bible.

"Emilie, the flour is sizzling."

Hurrying back, Emilie stirred the contents of the pan. They ate the mixture by the spoonful, as hot as they could stand it, washed down with hot water. They gazed at the empty pan awhile, without speaking. Then Emilie took up the turkey wing and swept the hearth.

"A clean hearth is a clean room," Otto chanted. His attempt at heartiness echoed in the silence.

"Remember you said you didn't want comfort, you wanted adventure?" Emilie said. "I think you can have both."

"What do you mean?"

"When Papa hauled you away after you sassed Frau Albrecht, the pastor said something I haven't forgotten: 'If God prevented all storms, when could He show you His comfort?'"

"So God will comfort us during storms?"

"That's what we say we believe. And now, with almost no food left, and not much wood, and no end to the storm in sight, we get to see if that comfort will hold us up. How much more adventure could you want?"

* * *

If we get out of this, God, I will tell Heidi Jurgen how real

You are, how You helped us, so she never doubts again ...

"Emilie!"

Feeling her shoulder jostled, Emilie woke from her dream. "The wood is gone."

"Start by burning the small stools, Otto. But we'll have to be careful now. We can't keep the fire as hot anymore."

Emilie knitted awhile, then paged through the Bible. What was that verse Frau Jurgen had quoted, when the women at the party worried over her? "'The Lord is my strength and my shield ...'" She turned more pages, running her hands over them as if her fingers could soak up the words.

"'And we know that all things work together for good to them that love God, to them who are the called according to his purpose.' Oh, Lord, I know that heavy drifts can block the roads, hurt the oxen, even kill people. Comfort Papa too, and Herr Schulz and his family, and the Jurgens, and the Zimmermanns...." The fire died down. She dozed again.

"Emilie!"

She roused.

"It stopped!"

She sat up, blinked.

"With the fire not roaring so loud, I realized I couldn't hear the wind anymore. So I looked. The sun is shining. The storm is over."

Emilie bolted to the door and gazed out. Over the carpet of white stretched a cloudless blue sky. "Thank You, God," she breathed.

"I'll shovel."

"We'll take turns," Emilie said. "We'll have to build up the fire to get warm in between." Reluctantly, Emilie sawed apart the last three-legged stool.

Otto followed her movements. "The storm might be over, but the adventure's not, is it?"

Emilie was just understanding this herself. "I guess the end of the storm is the first step. But the roads are buried. We don't know how long it will take Papa to come."

"What do we burn next?"

Emilie couldn't bear to burn more furniture. "The ladder to the loft," she decided.

As Emilie threw the wood onto the fire and straightened up, she felt faint. The feeling passed quickly, but she knew it was a warning. Watching Otto's small back bend with the thrusts of his shovel, she shut the door behind him and lifted her eyes to the gun rack. She knew what she had to do.

Chapter Eighteen

Dressed in her coat, mittens, and Papa's new scarf, Emilie stood on a chair and got the gun down.

"You're going hunting?" Otto's eyes bulged.

"Papa would. He can't help us now, but we're children of the King. He'll provide."

"Emilie."

She heard the fear in his voice, and looked back. "Otto, we need more food, and we need hot food. What if Papa's delayed? What if the storm starts up again?"

"What if you get hurt?"

"Papa could get hurt. He taught me to hunt for a reason. You remember how he divided the money among us on the trip?"

"Yes."

"Because it was smarter not to leave it all with one person. Hunting is the same. It's better not to leave it all to one person, because what if that person can't do it? Papa would want me to do this."

Otto's face wrinkled. "Don't be too long, Emilie."

"I won't stay out past dark. Pray, Otto. If you need to, start burning the ladder." She left the cabin.

Squaring her shoulders, Emilie stepped from the shoveled clearing into the deep snow. She wished she felt as confident as she'd sounded. Though a pretty good shot, Emilie worried about tracking animals, or scaring them away. She was operating on a dim idea that the snow might be less deep in the trees, and that animals might venture out by now to find food, just as she was doing.

Emilie entered a clump of trees. The snow did seem shallower, making her heart pump. A cold wind blew in her face, though, and penetrated her mittens. She'd have to find something soon, before her fingers got too numb to shoot. She glanced about, praying to see a brown smudge on the snow that might be a rabbit or squirrel. Nothing but twigs, trunks, and bark.

She searched until dusk, walking stealthily, running her eyes over the landscape. For a while she stood against a tree, trying to blend into its shape and color, and waited for something to come by. Nothing did.

It was too cold to stand still for long. Turning to put the wind at her back, Emilie followed her tracks toward the cabin. "Lord, maybe hunting isn't Your way," she prayed softly. "Maybe I should try digging for roots instead. But I will go into the woods at a different spot, one more time."

Then she turned to her left and saw it.

A deer.

Emilie froze, not daring to breathe. Thirty yards ahead, at the edge of the woods, the deer stood with its back to her, nibbling at bark. She turned her face to the slackening wind. The wind was in the deer's face, too. It could not smell her.

Mein Gott, she prayed, forming the words silently. She stole forward.

The deer lifted its nose and Emilie stopped still, heart thundering. *Don't let it run. I'm not sure I'm doing this right. Help me,* she prayed. The deer bent to the tree trunk again. Emilie stepped forward. She raised the gun, found the deer in her sights, shook off the mitten and squeezed the trigger as Papa had taught her to do.

Bam! The gun discharged and she staggered back, knowing if the shot had gone wild she'd lost her only chance. Frantically, she searched for the spot where the deer had stood.

A brown hump lay in the snow.

Emilie's legs went weak. "I did it. Oh, *mein Gott,* I did it. No, You did it. Thank You, thank You." She watched the deer. It didn't move.

She'd have to get it quickly, before some animal came to fight her for the carcass. Pulse beating, she looked from the deer to the cabin and back again. She could never haul the deer without Otto. But if they didn't hurry, they could lose their way in the dark.

Emilie plunged through the snow toward the cabin. "Otto! Otto!" She burst through the door. "Is there oil for the lamp?"

Otto leaped up from the fire. "You're back!"

"The lamp. Does it have oil?"

"You said you wouldn't hunt in the dark."

"Just light the lamp and set it on a stump. And I need a knife. I'll explain on the way."

Leaving the lamp gleaming to guide them, Emilie and Otto set out after the deer. The breeze had died down with the setting sun; they had to high-step through the snow, but the trek wasn't long. Excitedly, they knelt over the deer.

"I figure we should gut it here," Emilie said. "That will make it lighter to drag. And the insides might be food for animals." She paused, looking at Otto.

"Do you know what to do?" he asked.

"Besides slitting its belly, no," Emilie confessed.

"Just do the best you can," Otto encouraged.

"I'd hate to ruin good meat by doing something wrong," Emilie said, "but I guess I can't worry about that. Now that we have it, it'll at least keep us alive." She squeezed the knife handle, delaying the spill of hot blood and entrails on the snow. "I'd better get started. What if the lamp dies out before we get back?" They looked up, seeking the light.

This time they both went weak in the snow.

"The wagon?"

"No, a sleigh. A sleigh!"

"Papa!"

"But not only Papa. There are others." Too amazed to run screaming, Emilie watched as four figures alighted from the sleigh and approached the lamp on the stump. "Mama," she whispered, and then they were racing to the clearing. "Mama, Papa, Karl!"

"And Erich," yelled Otto. "Mama found them, just like she said she would."

They came together in a jumble of breathless shouts.

"What a wonderful welcoming light!" Mama clasped Emilie snugly. "Oh, *Liebchen.*"

"Emilie shot a deer!"

"Karl, you came! How . . . why . . . when . . ."

"We had to burn the stools in the fire!"

"Mama, you landed in Sheboygan before the blizzard started?"

"Yes. Herr Schulz's injury brought Papa to town, and then he heard we had come. God works in such wonderful ways."

"All things work together for good . . ." Emilie marveled. "Papa did bring something back for my birthday."

"And Herr Schulz's leg will be saved," reported Papa.

"But now that you're here," Otto yelled, "Emilie doesn't have to cut the guts out!"

Everyone laughed, and despite the warmth of their reunion made their way into the cabin.

The deer was taken care of and the fire built up. Mama brought out bread, dried meat, and fruit from town as she, Karl, and Erich told their story.

"I simply went back to our farm and the Jurgens' farm," Mama said, "let people know I was looking for Karl and Erich, and went on to Jena. In only a few days, praise God, I found them."

"I couldn't believe it," Karl said. Emilie gazed at his strong jaw in the firelight, at the new glow in his eyes. "I couldn't believe Mama had stayed behind for me."

"But we put her off at first," Erich continued. "For a month we tried university life, but had no money to enroll. Karl had no luck at coopering, since the wood for barrels cost more than the barrels sold for, and I had all I could do to earn a little food as a wagon maker. I had money saved up, but my pocket must have been picked somewhere." Erich shrugged. "I was broke."

"Oh, your pocket was picked, all right," Emilie said gently.

Erich looked startled. "You know about it?"

Emilie nodded. "Please don't ask me to explain. Your family will tell you. But your money is safe with them."

Erich's mouth dropped open.

"Maybe God does work things out," Karl said slowly.

"For those who love God, and are called according to His purpose," Emilie finished.

Karl held her gaze, then turned to Papa. "That's why I came. I don't know how much I trust God yet, and I don't know about His purpose. But poor as we were, we managed to scrape up money for passage. If God has a purpose, I'll at least try to listen. And the best way to listen must be to live with people who know how." He smiled faintly. "I missed you. I knew I would. I even sneaked into the women's room in Bremen to see them one last time."

"The closer to America we got," Erich added, "the more I couldn't wait to see my family."

"And I'll get you there right now." Papa stood.

"Erich?" Emilie called as the two started out the door.

Erich turned.

"Say to Heidi: 'Where your treasure is, there will your heart be also.' Promise me."

Mystified, Erich said, "All right. What does it mean?"

"It means," Emilie said, "whatever is worth most to us, that's what we love the best."

A knowing look came over his face. "And our treasure isn't always money, is it?" He nodded. "That statement is true."

"That statement is Scripture," she answered softly. "Goodnight, Erich. Give my love to Heidi, and everybody."

When the door closed, Emilie knew what other news she had to share. "The lusterware. It—didn't survive the trip."

"It broke?" Mama asked with disappointment.

"Almost all of it." She looked at Karl. "I'm sorry. It was your inheritance, and it's in pieces."

Karl shrugged.

"Except the cream pitcher. It's perfectly fine. Maybe because Heidi stuffed Erich's money in it."

"What?" exclaimed her mother and brother.

Quickly Emilie explained what she knew. "Unless God just kept that piece whole because—well, I don't know—because it somehow connected Heidi to Erich? And us to you?"

Karl said nothing, but she saw that her words had moved him. Spying the trunk against the cabin wall, Mama opened it and unwrapped the pitcher. She tipped it back and forth in the light, as Emilie and Louise had done on their last day in Thuringen. Its copper and blue finish shimmered.

"Karl's inheritance isn't gone," Mama said. She set the cream pitcher on the mantel above the fire. "Who knows, a single pitcher that once held a treasure may mean more than a whole set of dishes to eat off of."

"It can be our family's tie to Germany," Emilie said.

Mama smiled. "And how can we ever tell the story without being reminded of treasure in earthen vessels?" Mama opened her arms. Emilie, Otto, and even Karl hurried to embrace her.

"Herr Schulz will have more stories to tell now," Otto said. "Maybe the one about the girl who hid money in a cream pitcher. Or the boy and girl who survived alone in a blizzard. Or the girl who shot a deer."

"Or the mama and sons who followed their families over the ocean," Emilie added.

"Or the man who sawed his leg and didn't lose it. Herr Schulz will probably tell new stories all the time."

"So will we." Emilie grinned at him. "So will we."

Discover what coming to America
was like in these other exciting
Immigrants' Chronicles titles.

The Journey of Hannah
by Wanda Luttrell
ISBN 0-78143-082-8

When Hannah is brought to
America from the Sea Islands,
she is sold into a life of slavery.
After escaping from her cruel
surroundings and discovering
God's great love for her,
Hannah faces a decision that
could free her heart and
change her life forever.

The Journey of Pieter and Anna
by Helen DenBoer
ISBN 0-78143-083-6

Religious freedom draws
Pieter's family to America
from the Netherlands. Along
the way, they meet Anna, a
young girl traveling alone in
search of her father in
Michigan. Through helping
Anna, Pieter learns how much
we need God's help to help
and forgive others.